Image by Annis Taylor

Nell Haynes lives in the Kent countryside with her partner Paul, daughter Annis, future son-in-law Connor and her four much loved rescue cats.

To Annis and Lily x

Nell Haynes

CONDUIT

AUSTIN MACAULEY PUBLISHERS™

LONDON • CAMBRIDGE • NEW YORK • SHARJAH

A CIP catalogue record for this title is available from the British Library.

ISBN 9781398438972 (Paperback)
ISBN 9781398482302 (Hardback)
ISBN 9781398438989 (ePub e-book)

www.austinmacauley.com
First Published 2022
Austin Macauley Publishers Ltd®
1 Canada Square
Canary Wharf
London
E14 5AA

Conduit was a huge journey for me personally. One in which I discovered during my research the depths of the heinous human trafficking trade, a "rabbit hole" once entered can never be forgotten.

I extend my deep gratitude and love to Jaynie who kept me going when I didn't think I could. To Les and Lesley for their constant encouragement, ditto to Caroline and Rob.

Lastly, to Allan in the Azores, without your expertise *Conduit* would never have made it to the publishers.

Yours, Nell.

Luke 8-17 For nothing is hidden that will not be made manifest, nor is anything secret that will not be known.

1987

"Hi Nan, sorry I'm so late but the traffic was just dreadful."

"That's alright dear, you're here now and that's all that matters, I know how very busy you are. And what with your glamorous new job coming up I won't have you all to myself for our little tete a tetes for much longer, I shall so miss them."

"Now Nan, I'm a junior reporter, and Belgium by ferry isn't exactly glam but they've promised me if I do well, I might possibly get a chance of the American desk next year, and you know I will always find the time to spend with you. By the way there's some goodies in the bags along with the usual, oh and a nice bottle of Blue Nun."

"Oh, you naughty girl. Although I must say it's greatly appreciated and the wine just might help me sleep a little better."

"Don't say Granddad's snoring is keeping you awake; you do look rather tired."

"No my darling, it's so much more than that!"

"Now you're sounding a tad cryptic. Come on Nan we've always been able to talk to each other about anything and everything as well you know."

"Open the bottle of wine darling, I think the time has finally arrived for me to let you into a part of my life I've only ever shared with members of the spiritualist church, but my little kindred spirit may just understand."

"Well now I'm intrigued, I'll grab the glasses and the wine, get comfy then Nan."

What came next will stay with me forever.

Present Day

The pleas for help from earthbound babies and children to crossover to the heavenly realm started a few years ago for me, many, many years after that evening of revelation from my much loved and adored Nan.

During an evening of heartrending honesty, when Nan unburdened herself, telling me she possessed the ability to act as an "earth mother or conduit".

It had started happening to her decades ago, and only after a chance invite to a spiritualist church was the reason fleeting images of countless children's faces were flashing before her eyes practically every night been fully explained to her.

That she had been chosen to help these poor souls find peace and was not going crazy.

The faces she saw when in the twilight place between consciousness and sleep were in fact real souls, stuck between earth and heaven, that she was the channel to help them pass from one realm to another.

They were just fleeting glimpses of beautiful, pure little angels' faces, little ones who couldn't comprehend where they were or why.

It was the same for me, but Nan had always quietly said "I possessed the gift." How since from an early age she'd witnessed the growing signs in her youngest granddaughter.

That eerily I'd predict the presents Dad would bring me home from a business trip. Or when the doorbell rang I'd identify who was at the door, or totally out of the blue calmly telling Dad that Red Rum would win the Grand National.

The gift of sight had skipped a generation, landing firmly on my shoulders. A blessing at times, a curse at others.

I learned to block most of it, turn off the receptors if you like, but not the nightly twilight visits, so innocuous and innocent at first.

But you see it all started to change, the children were older now, and their pleas pitiful and desperate.

Recently they'd become more than visual visitations, increasingly vocal, mostly in French, Spanish and languages I didn't recognise. United in pleading with me to help children still alive, albeit trapped in terror and peril, in the most heinous conditions.

Dark, everything was so very dark, terrifyingly dark and the feeling of utter helplessness left me exhausted and shaken to my bones.

It was all so innocent before, and if I'm frank; easy, just close my eyes and let myself be used for the crossover, and it did feel wonderful knowing the peace it brought.

My life was relatively uncomplicated. I'd semi-retired, just writing the odd article, as and when I found a subject that caught my interest, no pressure for deadlines impeding my creativity.

I'd raised my children, with the youngest at university, the eldest two settled in their career paths. So, at last I had time to myself, taking up golf with the girls', playing badly I may add, leisurely lunches after, and I'd actually started yoga classes. No more juggling a career and the demands of three children.

Having finally hung up the "Mum's taxi" sign, ferrying them all to everything from judo to netball to horse riding. Standing in the freezing cold cheering on football matches and although I'd loved every minute of it, I now found myself thoroughly enjoying some me time.

Another bonus from all the above, being that Steve and I were finally getting away on our own too. Visiting all the places we'd promised ourselves we would when the children were old enough to not want to join us.

Places that didn't involve theme parks or any of their hobbies or my work. Having always been history buffs, Rome, Florence, Pompeii were top of our bucket list and we indulged ourselves.

Life was good and happy and everything I'd hoped it would be, but then my world changed beyond anything I could have or would have imagined. It became a maelstrom of emotions, from raw and unadulterated fear to the highest of highs, as I embarked on a journey to bring light from darkness and good from evil.

A journey that would be beyond dangerous, that would test my faith in humanity and God and draw on every ounce of strength I never knew I possessed, but tempered by the truly good and righteous souls I met along the way.

A journey at times so very frightening yet incredibly enlightening. My very own personal "road to Damascus".

My story is a devastating account that encompasses not only the very pits of humanity but the tremendous and far greater good there is too!

My innate need to share it is the only way I can pay tribute to the young ones who led me to search my soul, to garner the strength and embark on an insane mission to rescue the children. And to bring to public attention the silent war being waged against the scourge of human trafficking.

To bear the hurtful, albeit truthful, outbursts of my husband "that I was mad, that I'd hung up my investigative journalism hat, that I was too old," yet still I knew I had to do it, or I'd forever regret not trying. That as a Mum the instinct to protect the vulnerable is all empowering, all consuming. In short, I had to try.

One Year Ago, Chapter 1

"Aide-nous Manman, aide-nous Manman," is reverberating inside my head, my rusty French is enough for me to know that they are asking for, "help Mother." Every night for weeks it's been the same, enough for me to understand that something was terribly wrong somewhere, but where? Then in between aide-nous Manman I grasped ede nou Manman, with my investigative hat on I found that it was Haitian Creole, which narrowed down where the 'something terrible' was taking place.

Although I've travelled the world including many parts of the Caribbean, all I knew about Haiti was that it shared an island with the Dominican Republic, was quite a dangerous place, Papa Doc Duvalier had once been in charge with his militia the Tonton Macoute, voodoo was a way of life as the unofficial religion and that it had suffered a huge earthquake in 2010, and getting there was not easy nor recommended.

My old training kicked in immediately, research, research, research and when you think you've done enough research some more. Thank God and all that's holy for the internet, instant results. What came up immediately got my spidey sense in overdrive, connecting dots at an alarming rate, desperately trying to not draw instant conclusions. I was no Pulitzer prize winner, but I'd had reasonable success in my career and had a reputation for honesty and integrity, an attribute sadly lacking amongst many journalists today.

The same results kept coming up on my Google searches, results that left me reeling. Thousands of children left orphaned after the 2010 earthquake have literally vanished from the face of the earth and in a country where one in four people exists on $1.23 a day it wasn't hard to put two and two together and realise that the heinous and vile human trafficking trade was thriving in this poverty riven country.

That amongst all the confusion of the aftermath of the earthquake, it was perfect conditions for traffickers to pose as rescuers. It was becoming glaringly obvious these poor children were in more peril from supposed rescuers than a natural disaster.

I even read of organ harvesting, along with trafficking in human beings, these heinous acts a total anathema to me. Along with anger came utter revulsion and a burgeoning resolve to do something, anything, but the feeling of helplessness was overwhelming. What could a middle aged, suburban housewife possibly do to help?

The more I read the more I became convinced that I'd found a real link between the nightly imploring of the little ones to what I was discovering. I was slashing the odds of it all being a coincidence with each article I found, and I was quickly becoming obsessed with finding a way I could come to the aid of children in grave danger. I'm old enough and had been round the block enough to realise when huge sums of money were involved in something there would be layer upon layer of corruption and ultimately danger.

I started to feel so very alone, although Steve has always been an incredible listener and so very, very supportive, he's an everything has to be in black and white guy. With my journalistic background I was always the one who questioned things, I guess that's what made us such a good team. Steve being the solid, feet on the ground accountant, tempered my natural curiosity and need to question just about everything.

Chapter 2

However, there was someone with whom I could share my findings, someone who I know would see the connections and join the dots and not think I was turning into some conspiracy theorist.

Christian and I had been friends for years, since we'd both studied at Goldsmiths University, London. We met in Freshers week, hit it off straight away, he was just the most exciting person I'd ever met, well-travelled, spoke French like a native, loved red wine and debating anything and everything.

I think he in turn loved the fact I had a totally down to earth family, and would love nothing more than to retreat to rural Kent for weekends. My Mum's brother had inherited the family farm and although an agricultural one he still kept a well-stocked gun cupboard and loved to entertain my American friend to an afternoon of shooting.

I'd always had a love-hate relationship with guns, knowing the necessity for vermin control, but being a committed animal lover, the shooting of foxes and squirrels led to many family arguments.

My only concession was clay pigeon shooting, my Uncle had diversified some of his land to this and I admit to actually enjoying it. Couple all that with an absolute resolution to become journalists and good ones, it had led to a long lasting and treasured friendship.

Christian had been born in Beirut, his father a diplomat, stationed there for years and had fortunately been posted to the UK before the troubles and the siege in 1982.

The eternal bachelor had surprised us all by eventually marrying only a few years ago, an heiress to some world-famous railroad company. Though Christian had no children of his own, he proved to be a fantastic Godfather to my eldest son Jacob. Taking the role bestowed on him seriously and he relished in it.

Mentoring Jacob and smoothing his path to an internship with the newspaper where he was editor in chief, being just one of the many wonderful things Christian had arranged for my son.

This gateway to a career in US journalism however was short lived, Jacob being an independent soul, returned home after six months away. Wanting to make his way on his own merit his reasoning.

Back to describing my dear friend. Although my parents loved to take us abroad on holidays, nothing compared to Christian's travels around the globe, add in the American accent and the university honeypot was created.

The university lothario was only ever in my eyes at least, an incredible friend, Steve was my first and only love and fortunately the boys' hit it off too. In recent years we hadn't seen so much of each other as he'd landed the editors job at a major US newspaper, and now had a wife to consider too.

But without fail we spoke, emailed and skyped regularly. Both determined we'd never lose our precious friendship forged so many years ago.

We had also spent many happy family holidays together. Often at his family's stunning home in Kentucky, where now retired, his Dad indulged himself with breeding the most incredible horses.

I'd been around horses my whole life so when the boys' played tennis, and generally lapped up the whole American male sports thing, Lucy and I rode to our hearts content through some of the most beautiful countryside America has to offer, oh how I love the Bluegrass state.

We did however join them on adventures arranged by Christian, from white water rafting to camping out under the stars, a tad too survivalist for me, but the kids loved it.

Chapter 3

It was with a gigantic deep breath that I picked up the phone and dialled Christian's private line in Washington. I'd rehearsed exactly what I would say but still had massive doubts as to his reaction. What would he think of his old friend, her absolutely dark and sinister findings and not forgetting my inherited spiritual ability to be a conduit between realms?

I held fast to the fact that Christian had adored my Nan, and even though he is an agnostic of sorts he found it fascinating when she would produce her tarot cards and give him an impromptu reading.

I knew it was mostly out of respect and a helping of indulging her, as he always said when we die, "that's it, the final curtain and we turn to dust." I knew when she'd gotten something right though, which was often as Christian would become quiet and introspective, quite the opposite of his normal demeanour. So as much as I was certain he'd be onboard with my theories on the child trafficking and worse, he might find it hard to accept how I'd initially been stirred to investigate.

He answered on the fifth ring and I just went for it, barely coming up for breath. He allowed me to finish without interruption and there followed an awkward silence of several minutes before I plucked up the courage to ask if he was still on the line.

He was, thank goodness, and immediately went into investigative journalist mode. He asked that I email him all the information I'd amassed, that he would read it and report back asap. He had some big stories that were about to break and deadlines were looming, but after that he would read everything I sent over, assuring me he'd keep an open mind to everything.

True to his word, three days later my phone rang and it was Christian's number. He sounded different, almost furtive; I was instinctively alerted to his nuanced tone. With little or no preamble, he declared he was boarding a flight early that evening. Departing Dulles International airport and flying into Heathrow. He barely gave me chance to write the flight number down, before the phone line went dead.

Alarm bells were ringing, my shackles rising as different scenarios were playing out in my mind, my imagination in total overdrive. The overriding feeling was one of relief that he must believe what I'd sent him, because why else would a busy editor from a prominent newspaper be boarding a plane, flying for eight and a half hours to tell me it was all the findings of someone with an overactive imagination. No, he obviously had found my revelations to have some credence.

I couldn't wait for that bloody flight to land. Before then another hurdle had to be faced, this one involved telling Steve I'd gone behind his back, totally against his wishes and had carried on investigating something he'd told me to drop. Something he'd emphatically stated, "I didn't have a cat in hell's chance of doing anything about." Add to this I'd also enlisted the help of our dear friend and that friend would be arriving in just a few hours.

In all honesty I found telling Steve much, much easier than that initial phone call to Christian, my mind was made up and no one, not even my husband was going to stop me. The ensuing row wasn't pretty, but I stood my ground, outwardly strong and resolute, inwardly however was a different matter.

Bravado withstanding, I turned on my heel to get the spare room ready and nip to the supermarket to stock up on bacon, eggs and the ingredients for biscuits, the all-American breakfast staple, more scone than biscuit and utterly delicious. They were one of Christian's favourite foods and there was method in my madness, keep him fed and watered at home, away from any distractions.

From what I could gather during our brief telephone conversation, it was only going to be a flying visit, two days, but that surely would be enough time. I'd found even more conclusive evidence of heinous crimes against children and even an article concerning a doctor who after valiantly trying to expose child trafficking in his native Haiti, had travelled to the US only to be found murdered in his hotel room.

What were the chances of that happening? I was discovering far too many incidents relating to the sudden deaths of good and decent people suddenly dying as they tried to reveal evidence of the trafficking of children.

There was absolutely no doubt in my mind whatsoever now that I was onto something and that I had only just scratched the surface of the depths of depravity we would have to face.

Chapter 4

I parked the car, grabbed the ticket and made my way to the arrivals hall at Heathrow. I'd checked that Christian's flight was on time before I went to bed and once more before I left home, but still found myself checking the flight arrivals board, I suppose because there was still a tiny part of me that still couldn't believe he was on a plane due to arrive imminently. For the sole purpose of acknowledging in person whether or not I'd discovered/stumbled upon/been led by unknown forces to find and expose crimes against humanity.

As soon as I laid eyes on my friend walking into the arrivals hall, from the moment our eyes locked, I instinctively knew he believed me. Gone instantly were the worries about his initial tone and reaction during that first phone call. My friend and rock was here and the burden I'd been carrying immediately felt less heavy. That my gut instinct was right, that he would be the only one to see there was foundation to my strong belief, I was being used to bring revelation from unheard voices and pleas for help.

He engulfed me in his usual bear hug and then we proceeded to the car park, it was several minutes before either of us spoke. It was almost as if there was an invisible and tacit agreement that what we had to talk about was too sensitive for an arrivals hall and airport car park.

It was only when we were in the privacy of my car that the dam burst, both eager to check the other was ok and how genuinely pleased we were to be in each other's company again, although not for the usual happy reasons. With the pleasantries out of the way, I was the first to broach the subject of his visit:

"Do you believe what I sent you is true?" I hit him instantly with my burning question.

"Well I wouldn't be here Julia if I didn't, you hit a nerve, as we've been trying to cover human trafficking in general and the powers that be shut us down at every turn, yeh it's being reported on, but not the real deep dark shit my guys were unearthing."

I quickly replied, "Now you're sounding like what Steve was accusing me of being 'a conspiracy theorist', I was so bloody angry with him, he should know me so much better than that."

Christian was on a roll now replying, "Here's the thing though, yes it's a conspiracy but way not a theory, the conspiracy being the sick bastards complicit in the cover up, and it goes all the way to the top."

"When you say the top, what do you mean exactly?" my interest heightening exponentially.

"The very people we are taught at a young age to respect, Government officials, police officers, aid charities, the whole fucking lot and more," Christian added excitedly.

"Oh God, Christian, that's what I was beginning to fear, after I sent you the email I carried on digging. Whistle-blowers ending up discredited, their reputations in tatters or worse ending up dead."

"Look, even with my Old Man's connections we were starting to hit brick walls, sources normally good for inside information were backing off, it's a rabbit hole Julia."

"What do you mean, a rabbit hole?" I'd read the term during my research but welcomed Christian's interpretation of it.

"It's deep and has myriad tunnels reaching Christ knows where, but what I do know is once you're down it you have to carry on, and once you've seen what goes on, you're unable to unsee it."

"Is that why you hopped on a plane at more or less a moment's notice, you could have given me more of a heads up, that you believed what I was saying. You sounded so different after I'd revealed it."

"I think, no scrap that, I know some of my journos are being monitored."

"How do you know that for sure?"

"I had a visit a few months back from one of Dad's former security personnel at the Embassy in Beirut, he rose through the ranks and is due to retire soon, but out of respect for Dad wanted to warn me that certain people were aware of the papers digging."

"So, you backed off, right?"

"I'm ashamed to say it now, but yes, we backed right off, it was only after you contacted me with all the connections to children that my conscience got the better of me, kids for fucks sake."

"I know, I couldn't take it in at first, the images are pretty harrowing and the written testimonies of the few who have escaped are heart-breaking, I can't get them out of my head Christian, literally it's taking me over. Even when I try and sleep the little ones bombard me now."

"Hey, I'm glad you brought that part up, I gotta confess I found it difficult to get my head around it, why did you never tell me?"

"What, and have you think I'd lost the plot and how exactly could I have brought it up? Oh, by the way I've inherited my dead Grandmother's ability to act as some sort of channel for spiritual rest."

"Put like that I can see why, but come on I've been there when some pretty inexplicable and frankly weird things have happened around you and Clara, and man, I clearly remember some of those tarot readings!"

"You always seemed indifferent to that side of her, polite yes and indulgent but not exactly a believer."

"Yeah, by the way she got pretty close on a lot of things, but that's the past, I want to know about this conduit thing. I know you, and I also know you are one of the most honest and grounded people, so if you say it's happening, I believe you one hundred percent."

"It's no great reveal, I see faces of babies and children, they've always been silent until now. Fleeting glimpses, the

22

only way I can describe them is it's like those old cine films my Dad used to make where it's grainy and shaky and when it stops for the night, I have an all-encompassing feeling of peace."

Chapter 5

As I drove through the gates and onto the drive my stomach sank, Steve's car was sitting there, shit, he'd obviously decided to stay home. No prizes for guessing why! Not that I could blame him, he doesn't have a misogynistic bone in his body (we'd always strived to have our marriage be a partnership, where both of us were equally able to make decisions) but I had a strong feeling he was about to lay down the law.

When the front door opened before I'd even turned the car engine off my feeling of a gathering storm was confirmed. Steve's face was like thunder and Christian's response was epic "Jesus I feel like Clyde to your Bonnie," I smothered a giggle, even in such a profound situation he could still lift my spirits.

At least my husband had the good manners to take Christian's case, walk us both indoors, offer refreshments before he mounted his soapbox and began his lecture.

"Christian, as good as it is to have you here with us, what the hell are you doing flying all the way over here encouraging my wife in her insane idea that she can suddenly become the next Mother bloody Teresa."

"Whoa Steve, let's wind this back, firstly I'm not encouraging Julia in anything, I'm supporting her, and secondly, if I wasn't here she would without one shadow of a doubt go off on her own. Now I can't and won't let that happen, because she's onto something and it's beyond huge. The tip of an enormous iceberg of cruelty, depravity, greed and evil." I silently thanked Christian for that response.

"So what is it exactly that you are going to do then? Hop on a plane to Haiti, rescue these kids and ride off into the sunset as heroes." Steve's voice was dripping with sarcasm.

I interjected "Well that puts it in a nutshell love, yes that's what I intend to do, with or without your blessing."

"What about our kids then Julia, what do I tell Ethan, Jacob and Lucy, when they ask where their mum is? Off on a wild bloody goose chase in a country that is not only dangerous but lawless too." Steve wasn't giving an inch either.

Poor Christian was sat in the middle of a full-blown family meltdown, not surprising due to the gravity of the situation, he kept his counsel though and just let us slug it out. When finally Steve had run out of objectives and expletives, he started the case for the defence.

"Look Man, I'm well aware of how it must look, but firstly and of paramount importance is that you married an investigative journalist and a damned good one too. Yes, Julia has been out of the loop so to speak for a few years, but you know as well as I do that her op-eds go down a storm, she will always be a journalist, it's in her blood. And yes what we are talking about sounds fucking crazy, I see that loud and clear, but in all good conscience would you or could you not react in any other way when kids are involved, for heaven's sake?"

Steve didn't hold back. "Don't make me out to be some unfeeling, cold and selfish sod Christian, that's below the belt and you know it. But this is my wife who is potentially putting her life in danger, the mother of my kids, my soulmate."

"Well, whilst you two are acting as if I'm not in the bloody room, I'll cook brunch shall I. You know Steve like the good wife and Mother, and then Christian and I are going to plan our trip."

With that I left the room, made for the kitchen, normally the heart of my happy home, today even the dog and cats scattered in various directions from the warmth of the Aga. My loved and trusted pets were giving me a wide berth, I couldn't blame them, my mood was blackening by the minute.

Chapter 6

I heard the front door open and close as Christian entered the kitchen, he didn't have to tell me that Steve had obviously gone to the office. Good, it would give us a chance to eat and plan in peace without negative comments and an ever-expanding cloud of impending doom descending on the pair of us. Christian did start to defend Steve, but I refused to acknowledge this act of brotherly solidarity and fired up my laptop.

First class air travel does indeed have its blessings as Christian had slept most of his flight over from Washington, ergo he declined my suggestion of a nap and appeared eager to see what else I'd discovered since my initial email.

Perhaps he was already onboard and all my worries about having to convince him were unfounded, and again the thought came into my mind that he wouldn't have flown all this way to debunk my theories in person, when he so easily could have done so over the phone.

However, there was one burning question I had to ask, a question that had been on my mind since the phone call informing me he was dropping everything and coming over. As he was unpacking his laptop I went straight for it:

"How did Candace take the news that you were travelling here? You know with her social calendar always being so jammed with the old black-tie bashes and charity fundraisers, I know you are booked up for months in advance." Trying to make light of one of the elephants in the room, I'd had nagging worries in recent months that things weren't good in the Dupont household.

He'd not said anything but my intuition was rarely wrong, especially with people close to my heart which Christian undoubtedly was. Nevertheless I was taken aback with his response.

"I was wondering when you'd broach the subject, surprised actually that it's taken you this long!" He suddenly looked weary and every one of his 55 years, gone instantly the debonair, confident well-bred son of a wealthy diplomat, the man sitting opposite me looked vulnerable, one of the rare times since I'd known him.

"The situation hasn't been good for a while, you know that saying, marry in haste and repent at leisure, well that pretty well sums up how I find my life is at the present moment," Christian sadly replied.

I didn't pass comment, only nodded or shook my head at the appropriate time. I just let him open up, quickly realising that he sorely needed someone to listen, that that someone wouldn't judge him. I only felt sadness that he hadn't confided in me before this trip.

He revealed many things, how vacuous his marriage had been, one long schedule of being seen at the right places with the right people, photographed for the right magazine. I knew that Candace being an heiress, they moved in uber elevated circles, but he always appeared comfortable with it.

In all honesty I couldn't say a bad word about Candace, with us she had always been the perfect hostess, charming and welcoming. Also, a control freak without a shadow of a doubt, but I suppose having a few million bucks in your trust fund could make you that way. But what Christian said next did shock me and induced a twinge of guilt at wanting to get to the reason for his sitting in my kitchen and it wasn't his marital problems.

"At first the philanthropic part was good. I'd been used to it my whole life with Dad as you know. But in the last year or so it started to evolve into some real creepy, weird and deep shit. More and more I used the newspaper as an excuse to not being able to attend functions and Candace just got angrier each time."

My curiosity was well and truly piqued now and I couldn't help myself, I had to ask. "What do you mean by that last sentence? Creepy, weird and deep shit has my imagination at defcon bloody one."

"You have to swear to God not to repeat this Julia. It was made pretty goddam clear to me that what happened at these gatherings stayed at these gatherings."

The hairs on the back of my neck started to rise as this dear and always supremely fearless friend actually looked and sounded scared. "Ok I swear to my God not to repeat what it is you're going to tell me, but please just bloody well tell me."

"The first time was at a private fund raiser for some guy running for Congress, by the end of the night the dude had pretty damn well pledged virtually everything including his firstborn in return for election to Congress. At one point Candace, her Father, brother and several other mega-wealthy donors went into a separate room with the guy, they said it was to write cheques and stuff, but I'm not convinced it was, because he came out sweating like the proverbial pig. Looked like he was getting ready to upchuck the lobster and Chateaubriand he'd stuffed his face with."

I calmly replied, "Well yes, I can understand that that situation would make you feel uncomfortable Christian, but come on it's hardly earth shattering is it, I've always been of the strongest opinion that most politicians or wannabe politicians had a price where they'd sell their grannies to the highest bidder, politics corrupts and very few can resist it. We've covered it enough during our careers and you are in the heart of the vipers nest, Washington DC. I'd have thought that there was little that would shock you, rather like the scabby lot over here, I wouldn't trust the majority of them with Lucy's guinea pig, all self-serving narcissists if you want my brutally honest opinion."

"As ever Julia, you sum everything up succinctly and to the point my friend, and yes I am well aware of the inner machinations of corruption in Governments, but you know before it was college fund for kids or a condo in Nassau or paying off some sex scandal, in exchange for future favours and we all know it's been going on since forever. But recently it's become pretty self-evident that a lot of people in DC are being leveraged, a lot of favours being called in."

"Are you doing an exposé on it?"

"We tried but got shut down almost immediately on orders from the top, the new breed of wealthy newspaper owners are overtly political and don't give a damn who knows it, gone are the good old days of good and proper journalism with impartiality, now it seems they all have a covert agenda and it's not for the good of the masses, their readership, they just want to brainwash people with their leftist crap."

"OK, I can see you're deeply unhappy and disillusioned and I feel like crap that I didn't know this beforehand, that you obviously didn't feel you could confide in me, but how does this all correlate with my contacting you with my belief that thousands of children are being trafficked or worse, much much worse?"

"It doesn't but perhaps it serves a need in me to get the hell out of the swamp and do something worthwhile with my life. Your phone call was like a lifeline to me, cathartic almost and I truly believe a Godsend, though these days God seems a dirty word in DC, you're more likely to Goddamn well hear the word Moloch than you are the Lord's name."

"Crikey, I've got goosebumps all over now Christian, when I was researching the missing children there were several references to exotic islands with tunnels and temples to Moloch or Baal, child sacrifice and quite a body of thought that some of these trafficked kids end up there."

"I read some of that too, but with in-laws who do actually own a private island in the Caribbean I tried to put those thoughts out of my mind, I've only ever visited a few times but Candace flies out regularly, she says she goes to be rejuvenated, whatever the hell that means."

"How the one percent live eh, but on a serious note she never mentioned that, you know the island." I couldn't help but add in astonishment.

"I think it's kept for oligarchs, politicians, a good assortment of Hollywood and the music industry, apparently it's where they can go to relax without the hoi polloi bothering them and no doubt organise their next charity fundraiser for the little people in need."

"I can see why you wouldn't go often, that's not you at all, you and your family are far more discreet."

"Thank you, and yes that's one of the reasons I rarely went, sycophants make me nauseous. Anyway, here I am ready, willing and at your service Ma'am." Christian quickly and deftly changed the subject of discussion.

"My dear friend you cannot possibly ever understand how truly grateful I am to hear those words, but you are such a busy man with so many commitments, how can you spare the time?"

"I decided on the flight over here to take a sabbatical, I think I deserve it. I'm going to announce my intention to write a book, every man and his dog is doing it, so it'll be a good cover story."

"Does that mean you are going to travel to Haiti with me then?" My voice rising with anticipation of Christian's answer.

"Well if you think I'd let you go by yourself, you're very much mistaken. I think you have stumbled onto something gargantuan and I'm not going to sugar coat it, we have the fight of our lives on our hands. But I have my contacts and my Dad's too, so I'll be calling in a few favours no doubt."

I excitedly replied "I think we're going to need all the help we can get, you've read the research I sent you, it's highly organised with massive bribery and corruption, how else can these children just simply disappear. It started in the aftermath of the earthquake, utter devastation and confusion made easy bedfellows for the traffickers to descend on the vulnerable. But it continues to this day because they're dirt poor and nobody would believe them even if they did question it. Promises of a better life with a few dollars thrown in to ease their decision must seem like a gift from God."

"Roger that Julia, and you're right, the cover up does go to the top, how else can this have remained covered up for so long? these people are beyond sick. It was bad enough reading about the sex trade but organ and blood harvesting put everything on a whole new level of wickedness."

I was eager to share more of what I'd unearthed. "Whilst I was researching the trafficking angle, I discovered so much corruption. Did you know that Haiti has vast mineral and gold reserves and the rights to these reserves have been sold to US interests and that there was a massacre on the 6th July 2005 and many believe the UN carried it out?"

Christian had obviously been digging too as he replied "Most of Joe Public believe that the earthquake was the only catastrophe to befall Haiti, but believe me that country has been pillaged for years. Venezuela gave a $4 billion loan and it literally disappeared, then US sanctions against Venezuela blocked Haiti from repaying a Petrocaribe oil loan, so in 2017 Maduro authorised the use of $85 million of the funds be used to revive agriculture, the gangsters stole it."

I added for good measure "Oh my God, these poor people, I read that even their rice production was sabotaged by cheaper imports, and yet the people are starving, it's actually becoming hard to comprehend the level of stinking rotten corruption. I think we've only just scratched the surface of what this poor Country has endured."

"Yes, it's happening worldwide and the research always leads back to a select few organisations, it's a global cabal without doubt. That segues into my main concern and that's our safety once we're over there," Christian sagely added.

"From what we've been discussing can your Dad's contacts rustle up a navy seal team, and I'm not jesting."

"Funny you should mention them, there have been several ex-seals found to be working for the black hats or bad guys over there, posing as the good guys, sick or what, the rabbit hole goes deep." Christian shook his head as he imparted this information.

"OK, now you're beginning to scare me Christian, I know perhaps I've been somewhat naive and blinkered with my obsession to find these children, I knew there'd be danger, but this is spiralling into something far beyond anything I could have imagined."

"We certainly have a herculean mission on our hands Julia, and I will admit it feels insurmountable but what is the alternative? I go back to Washington, you carry on with your life, we try and forget the kids. I don't think either of us could live with that, we can't unsee what we've seen and unread what we've read can we?" Christian implored.

Chapter 7

Following all these revelations I can't with hand on heart say I felt better, but my resolve was still set in stone, no one was going to stop me now. Christian and I had decided on a plan of action, it felt almost surreal, like something out of a Tom Clancy novel.

My life was about to take a paradigm shift, literally turn on its axis and I was calm, unbelievably calm. I could attribute most of my state of mind to the fact that Christian was on board, lock stock and barrel, but there was also an integral part of me that intrinsically knew that I also had others on my side too, the little ones who had led me on my very own road to Damascus.

We had decided on an outline plan, a strategy for our mission. Christian would return home and sort out his affairs, which could take a couple of weeks. As he insisted, he'd have to make sure there was a smooth transition for the new editor.

Thankfully his deputy was more than capable of stepping into the role with little notice or fanfare. Next, smooth things over with Candace and explain the book cover story, and that to concentrate on this new venture he would need to be away from D.C. and all its distractions to get his literary juices flowing. He'd insisted that Candace not be told of the real reason behind this dramatic change in careers. I thought it strange that the person he was closest with wouldn't be privy to our trip, but I had so much going on inside my head, the thought didn't linger long.

He would then travel to Kentucky, to his Father's estate and explain everything. We needed Mr Dupont senior on board, for his contacts and connections, visas etc, but also to ask that he covered for Christian's book writing facade. We would need his Dad to keep up the pretence of Christian writing his book there in Kentucky, but also he might undertake travelling for research purposes. The perfect cover for Christian being incommunicado at times.

From Kentucky Christian would fly to the Dominican Republic, I would meet up with him there, then we'd travel together to Haiti.

To avoid suspicion we would spend a couple of days in Santo Domingo, posing as regular tourists, before crossing the border and heading for our destination of Port au Prince and the American Embassy.

That was the straight forward part, everything after was in the hands of the Gods and whoever we could find to help us along the way.

In the meantime, I had to get my vaccinations up to date, I was ok for typhoid, hepatitis A&B and cholera but my polio and tetanus needed updating, so while Christian showered, I made a quick call to my local GP and booked my shots. I couldn't book my flight until Christian returned home and had a definite time scale for what he had to do.

So that only left telling my family of my impending trip, I'd decided to ask Steve to leave out the true reason, that my cover story was Uncle Christian had asked me to accompany him on a fact finder for the book he was finally going to write.

I refused to cause my children any unnecessary or premature stress and prayed Steve would go along with my being economical with the truth. He was due home imminently, so I poured Christian and I a large glass of Dutch courage while we waited, the Malbec worked, I was calm, relaxed and ready when Steve came through the door.

I really don't know what happened between him walking out the door that morning and returning home, but Steve's whole demeanour and attitude had taken a three-hundred-and-sixty-degree shift, and it was a positive shift too.

Gone was the angry man, it was almost as if he had admitted defeat to himself. I guess it stemmed from years of marriage to a headstrong and equally as stubborn woman. A woman who although a loving, loyal wife and Mother,

34

adopted bloodhound mode when I was on the scent of a good cause, and although I'd been out of the loop for a while, I'd never lost my enthusiasm for investigative journalism.

All that combined and culminated in a mature and calm discussion between the three of us. Much to my astonishment Steve agreed to Ethan, Jacob and Lucy being told only the bare bones for the reasons of my impending trip. That I'd been invited by Uncle Christian to help him on a foreign assignment, that he needed someone with experience of international human rights abuses.

I'd covered the burgeoning Balkan crisis from 1991, undertaking a couple of short stints to the Belgrade office of my newspaper up until war broke out in April 1992. I'd reported on the siege of Sarajevo and was still haunted by the images of that time, of heinous human rights abuses. I'd also heard unconfirmed but reliably sourced rumours that human trafficking was being aided and abetted by the most respected of the global organisations.

The very same organisations mandated to oversee and ensure the safety of the victims of the war. Ergo why I had a deep seated and I feel vindicated distrust of IGO's (intergovernmental organisations) and let's add some NGO's (non-governmental organisations) into the mix too.

My Grandfather was in the Royal Navy during the second world war and my Great Uncle in the RAF. I can remember them both often saying that after the Holocaust, genocide must never be allowed to happen on European shores again, but it did happen and it happened in the Balkans.

I'd only spent a short time out there, but it was long enough to learn of the terrible things one human being could inflict on another, without conscience and how in the midst of war, there were many that would see this as a lucrative time. As vile concept as it is, it happened and is still happening.

Not long after this I married Steve and within a couple of years our first child Jacob had arrived and although my life had taken a totally new direction, my priorities changed, I would never forget my first experience of human rights abuses and what terrible injustices one human being was capable of inflicting on a fellow member of the human race.

Chapter 8

Joshua 1-9
Have I not commanded you?
Be strong and courageous,
Do not be terrified
Do not be discouraged
For the Lord your God will be with you wherever you go.

Eleven days after Christian returned to Washington DC and I was on my way to Heathrow airport for my 2p.m. flight to Punta Cana. The only way I can describe the atmosphere in the car was surreal, a journey we'd made so many times before. Just the two of us or with the family. Journeys that were always full of chatter, laughter and excitement all rolled into one, but now we talked about everything but the purpose of my trip.

Me telling Steve to remember to give the dog her medication each morning, check in on our recently widowed neighbour, make sure Lucy's monthly allowance was transferred to her bank account, not to forget to leave out Mary the cleaning lady's money. Anything but my impending foray into the unknown, that was until we arrived at the short-term parking, when he grabbed hold of me so tightly I struggled to breathe. Years of love and companionship manifesting into this physical display of emotion. I struggled to hold back the tears that threatened to shatter the armour of strength I'd enveloped myself in, Steve wasn't so stoic, the tears falling down his cheeks. I'd only ever seen him cry when our children were born. The levity of his emotion hit home, was I being a selfish bitch? I could be sacrificing everything we had, to travel halfway round the world on a spiritual hunch.

I was travelling light, just a small pull along case, a holdall and my backpack, but Steve still insisted on transporting it to the check-in desk, ever the courteous gentleman I loved deeply. We kissed briefly before I pulled away and walked to baggage check and passport control. I only looked back briefly, afraid that I would have a change of heart and run back into his arms, but Steve was already walking away, back to the car, back to our home, back to our normal but oh so cherished life.

I had an hour before my flight, my stomach was in knots after the display of emotion in the car park, I couldn't eat but found myself sitting at a bar ordering a large glass of Malbec, just waiting for my gate to be announced on the display board.

A middle-aged man plonked himself down on the bar stool next to mine, and as I took another sip of wine he started to strike up a conversation. I tried to give him my best 'I'm busy' look as I pretended to check something on my phone, it didn't work. He asked me where I was travelling to, I casually said, "The Caribbean," but my internal radar went to defcon one, when he just looked me straight in the eyes and said, "the Dominican Republic and Haiti can be very dangerous places," downed the whiskey he'd ordered, casually put a ten-pound note on the counter and walked off.

I know I'd drunk a large glass of wine on an empty stomach, but I still retraced the last few minutes in my mind, I definitely hadn't mentioned my exact destination, how did he know? And the way he'd said it, cold and matter of fact but without doubt a threatening undertone.

I went straight to the ladies toilets and my hands trembling dialled Christian's phone. I tried to keep calm but it didn't work as I relayed what had just taken place. His reply was brief, "Put the phone down, do not use it again and we will discuss this at our rendezvous."

By now my flight was being called, I hurried to the gate, showed the necessary paperwork at the desk and waited for my row to be called. Once seated I tried to take stock of the situation, but my brain was in overdrive, and even in my agitated state I quickly came to the conclusion that before we'd even arrived in Haiti, there were people who knew why and where we were heading to, but how on earth did they know?

I tried to comfort myself with the knowledge that Christian was well connected and protected by some pretty powerful people himself, that he would have the situation under control. I realised I was placing a hefty responsibility on his shoulders, in truth I was desperately trying to convince myself that everything would be ok, that I'd be safe and protected with him by my side.

I attempted to watch an inflight movie but couldn't concentrate. Resorting to my iPod and my favourite playlist, even that didn't hold my attention for long. So, I popped a couple of calming tablets and tried to sleep. Thank God they worked for a few hours, I then played a dust up your French download on my iPod, and finally heard the magic words from the cockpit "cabin crew prepare for landing." The nine hours had seemed and felt like an eternity.

I knew exactly what I had to do once I'd cleared passport control and retrieved my luggage from baggage reclamation. Proceed to the arrivals hall, locate a driver who would be holding a card with my name on it, follow him to the awaiting car that would take me to the hotel. Once there I was to check in, go to my room and wait for Christian to arrive. I did exactly that and as I had a few hours to kill, I showered, got a coke from the minibar and sat on the balcony watching life carry on two floors below me.

I must have dropped off to sleep as I awoke to hammering on my room door and Christian calling my name. I hurried to open it and felt a huge wave of relief to see my friend standing in front of me. Although surprise fought with the relief as Christian was not alone.

Both men entered the room before Christian introduced his companion. "Julia, this is Raul." I'd barely shaken hands as Christian announced a change of plan.

We weren't staying in the hotel overnight, the change of plan involved us leaving immediately for the border, Raul and he would take my luggage down the back staircase. I was to leave by the front lobby door, take my time though and make it look as if I were just going out for the evening.

This would give them time to bring the car round to the front of the hotel, not before I rang home and let Steve know I'd landed safely adding that Christian had arrived and we would shortly be leaving for the border.

Trying to be as nonchalant as possible, just pretending to be your average tourist as I waved back to the sweet girl on reception and bade her "bonsoir" in return. I was still in the revolving door when I clocked Christian and Raul in a black SUV that wouldn't have looked out of place on an episode of an American crime show. I hopped in the back and our journey to the border began.

Chapter 9

Ephesians 5:11
Have nothing to do with the fruitless deeds of darkness,
but rather expose them.

Raul had barely pulled away and into the traffic before I asked Christian a litany of questions, starting with what was the reason for the change of plan and leaving immediately for the border and more importantly and worryingly what the bloody hell did he think had transpired between the guy at the bar in Heathrow and I. He took off his seat belt, turned in his seat enabling him to look straight at me before answering.

"Firstly, it's safer to change plans at the last minute, that way we are one step ahead, and secondly the guy at Heathrow was obviously sent to scare you off."

"But how can anybody know of our trip, let alone the fact that I was travelling to the Dominican Republic then onto Haiti, Christian I don't mind admitting it's frightened the fuck out of me and we haven't even arrived in Haiti yet!" I quickly replied.

"I can only imagine how intimidating the encounter at Heathrow must have been for you, as to how he knew, I have a few ideas and so does Raul, who by the way is ex-special forces." The last part of Christian's sentence had my interest piqued.

"Well Raul I am incredibly pleased to meet you and beyond relieved to hear of your credentials, may I ask what branch of special forces?"

"Ma'am, I'm pleased to make your acquaintance too. I was honoured to serve as a navy SEAL for eight years, I was born in the US of Haitian parents, hence my eligibility to serve as a SEAL, and my right to dual citizenship. Sadly, to live

41

here I had to renounce my US citizenship, it was very hard for me as the US had given me so much, but I believed I could help the country of my ancestors, so I joined the Haitian police force," Raul explained.

"OK Raul, firstly please call me Julia and secondly, that's very impressive and also a first for me as I have never met a navy seal before, ex or current. Secondly your altruism is to be admired, it must indeed have been a tough choice to make. So, guys, what conclusions have you arrived at regarding the message from Blofeld at the airport?" I quipped.

"It's good to hear your British sense of humour is still intact Julia, Christian retorted but on a serious note my take on all of this is that human trafficking is on such a massive scale that it pervades all walks of life. We are in no doubt that algorithms exist on most search engines and when Joe public does their internet searches, these algorithms are set to catch certain key words. Ergo, in your searches you obviously used keywords that are set to alert certain groups with nefarious intentions and big connections, their tentacles reach far and wide and I should add deep too."

"But what have certain search engines got to do with human trafficking? I can't for the life of me see a connection between the two, oh shit wind that last comment back, are you surmising that figures from these companies may in some way be connected to human trafficking?" My tone one of genuine surprise.

Raul cut in, "Got it in one, and that's the consensus of opinion amongst a lot of us, and its gaining traction. That's why when Christian made contact and asked for my take on your research I literally bit his hand off to join you both."

Impressed, I added "You sound as if you know a whole lot more about this than I do, but I'm curious now as to how you two know each other?"

"I got to know Christian via his dad and some diplomatic work I was involved with a few years ago, and let's just say we are politically and ethically in tune." Raul obviously didn't want to expand further and I wasn't going to push the subject, but I did have a lot of burning questions.

"Now I know why the need for leaving the hotel the way we did, to throw anybody who may be trailing me off the scent, so what's the plan now?" I asked.

Raul then asked me a question, that rather threw me, a curve ball so to speak. I'd assumed and for the life of me I don't know why, that Christian wouldn't have mentioned my nightly visits from the spiritual realm.

"Julia, I've been raised a strong Catholic, but with what I've witnessed, the inhumane cruelty that one man can inflict on a fellow human being, its led me to question my faith, and then Christian mentioned your initial reason for starting all this and I've got to say I'm absolutely fascinated by your for want of a better explanation 'gift'. Truly you have a gift, one day maybe you will explain it at length to me."

"I will Raul, but there isn't much to explain really, I inherited my Nan's ability to help children in spiritual limbo, that's it short and sweet."

"Yes, I get that, but it has gotten kind of more than that now, with these kids asking you to help kids that are still alive."

"Believe me Raul, I was at a total loss initially, especially with the language changing and the fact that they were no longer silent entreaties, but very much vocal, I didn't question it for one moment and the rest they say is history."

Over the next hour I learned that false papers had been obtained for me, passport, visa, and driver's license, I was now to be known as Linda Grey, an archaeology professor from the UK and I was travelling to Haiti to participate in historical digs, as part of a doctorate I was working on.

Christian's cover was equally as academic, he would be posing as a fellow professor. It was his university in the US that had undertaken the financing of the trip.

Apparently, we had worked together on field trips to Iraq and Ethiopia amongst other places. I had to memorise and remember a whole lot of facts, dates and times. Raul's cover being he had been brought along for security purposes, the only truthful part in this spiders web of cover that had been meticulously woven and of which I had been blissfully unaware.

I didn't question or want to know how all this subterfuge had been arranged. I just felt a little safer that we had good, concrete cover, well at least I hoped and prayed we did.

I assumed a lot of help had been garnered from the US Embassy in Port au Prince, it's not what you know, but who you know sprang to mind, but I was informed enough, especially through my hours of research, that for every good guy, there'd be a bad one somewhere waiting in the wings. Christian and Raul had alluded to this often during my 'pep talk'.

During our conversation I mentioned I'd completed a Krav Maga course, which seemed to impress Raul. Adding I'd insisted Lucy do it when she was studying her A Levels and in time for when she applied for university. She hadn't been keen and only agreed if I did it with her, and I relished every class, even urging friends with teenage daughters to enrol too.

Having two older brothers had toughened my little lady up, but they'd been raised to always respect that she was not only younger, but not as physically strong as them, the boys had inherited their Dad's height luckily, whereas my beautiful daughter was 5.5ft like her mum.

I recalled the giggles and protests of pain on our drive home from the Krav Maga classes, it all seemed a million miles away from where I sat now, on my way to goodness knows what!

As it was some 250 miles to the border Christian and Raul had time to give me a crash course in my new identity, and fired questions at me to ensure I'd taken it all on board. Luckily, they had brought supplies with them, so we ate and drank in the SUV and I managed to grab some much needed sleep. Comfort breaks were taken on the road side, thank goodness for trees and darkness.

Chapter 10

Christian woke me about twenty minutes from the border and reminded me to speak only when spoken to, and to defer to him if possible, in layman's term, let him do the talking. I was more than happy to go along with that as my nerves were starting to get just the tiniest bit wrangled.

We'd made good time and had a couple of hours to kill as the checkpoint didn't open until 8a.m.. So we stopped off at a little street cafe set amidst a busy market, Christian ordered whilst I located what passed for a rest room and managed to clean my teeth, brush my hair and just generally tidy myself up.

By the time I arrived back at the table some very strong-smelling coffee and snacks were waiting, we all dived in and for a short while it did actually feel like we were just three friends on holiday together.

The guys had decided to cross the border at Jimani-Malpesse, the reason being it's the largest, busiest and most organised of all the border crossings. They explained that if indeed I was being tracked, they'd expect me to cross at a quieter less prominent place, so they were literally hiding me in plain sight. Good thinking indeed.

The change in my identity should also help too, apparently and luckily there were few if any security cameras for anyone to hack and track me visually. They had thought of everything, down to the tiniest detail.

The need for special authorisation by car had already been obtained, so in theory it should be a straight forward entry in to Haiti and then approximately another hour by road before we reached our destination of Port au Prince. The border crossing was uneventful thankfully.

Christian had arranged three rooms at a small guest house situated on Route de Freres, his reasoning being that it would be more "under the radar" than the three of us turn up at an international hotel with lots of eyes and ears. He also hadn't ruled out the possibility we might stay at the Embassy at some point too.

I didn't argue, everything so far had made sense, after my encounter at Heathrow the guys were obviously thinking of every possible scenario.

My leaving the hotel in Punta Cana so quickly, in darkness and my new identity papers would hopefully be enough to confuse any would be trackers.

Raul parked the SUV, we gathered our baggage, and proceeded to check in at the guest house. It would suit our purposes, three adjoining rooms, a bathroom, communal kitchen, access to a rooftop terrace and most importantly tucked away behind large trees and what could pass as an ornamental garden.

I saw Christian hand over a wad of extra dollars and surmised that was hush money if anyone should come asking questions. I pulled him up on it as I opened my room door to drop off my luggage, and his answer was short "money talks here Julia, that guarantees no loose lips."

I was cool with that, in fact I had to stop and take stock of the situation, just for a minute.

I was actually here in Haiti, I almost pinched myself to make sure I wasn't dreaming. I'd always had the ability to compartmentalise my work, home life, personal feelings from professional feelings, but now found my emotions were all blurring into one, with no definition between them. I knew I had to keep a clear head and just concentrate on what I'd come here to accomplish.

We regrouped in Christian's room 10 minutes later to discuss the plan for the rest of the day.

It had been mentioned during our road trip that Christian's Father had arranged for security clearance to get us in to the US Embassy and meet with certain officials and a Haitian human trafficking expert. I should have felt positive that things were moving quickly, however why were alarm bells ringing in my brain, had I read too many articles where the good guys turned out to be the bad guys? I just wanted as few people as possible knowing our plans, surely the tighter the circle, the less likelihood of leaks!

I was definitely falling prey to paranoia or was there more to it, was I picking up on some subconscious message? A message that I couldn't decipher, perhaps because my brain was on overload at the moment, maybe tonight I would use some of the yoga relaxation techniques I'd recently learned to relax, open my mind and see what came through.

Chapter 11

We were on the move again in the SUV, winding our way to the American Embassy situated on the Boulevard du 15 Octobre. It was only a short journey but as there had been yet another security alert of armed men in the area, all Embassy staff had been told to stay inside the personnel housing compounds or the Embassy itself.

As we neared the compound Christian's mobile rang, from what I could make out the call was from his contact and he was being given instructions for our arrival, in return Christian gave him the SUV's registration number.

Raul was obviously used to being in this kind of situation as Christian didn't need to tell him what to do. He drove straight up to the uniformed armed officers at the checkpoint, wound down his window, offered our paperwork which was waived away.

One of the armed officers glanced inside, obviously checking the three of us out, then he spoke into his radio and the security barrier was raised. Next were large gates, which opened on our approach and voila we were inside the Embassy.

I noticed a man coming down the front steps and heading towards us, Christian warmly shook hands and introduced him as William Monroe, the Ambassador.

He welcomed us to Haiti and then led us up the steps and into the Embassy. We were shown into what I can only describe as a conference room with a huge wooden table, a copious number of chairs, and two beautiful star-spangled banners stood either side of a very large screen.

The door opened again and a uniformed man entered, William Monroe introduced him as Captain Daniel Baptiste of the Haitian National Police.

After the introductions were over, we seated ourselves at the table and William Monroe kicked off the meeting:

"It's good to have you guys here, Christian it's been a while since we've seen each other and how's the Old Man?"

Christian smiling replied, "He's good thank you, and yes it certainly has been a while. I'd like to thank you, William, for meeting with us and smoothing our entry into Haiti, we all are so very grateful, especially as we had to bring it forward at such short notice."

William Monroe replied, "Well after you called and told me about Julia's encounter at the airport, I gathered you would, frankly I'm not surprised in the least at what took place. But I have to ask do you guys understand what you are getting yourselves into? Child trafficking is a very big and a very lucrative business, spread worldwide and an extremely dangerous one too. You are not the first who have tried to do something, believe me, and a lot have ended up dead."

I couldn't help myself and dived into the conversation.

"Mr Monroe, please do not take this the wrong way as I am so profoundly grateful for your assistance so far, but Christian, Raul and I are only too painfully aware of the dangers that getting involved in this spider web of evil involves, anyone with a computer can within minutes use their search engine and find masses of information and leave it right there, however as a strong believer in right and wrong, once I became aware of the pain and torture many of these children are subjected to, I for one could not sit back and do nothing."

"I copy that Julia, our intel is providing some pretty heinous information and Haiti has provided rich pickings for these sick bastards for too long, one helluva a blind eye was turned to what was going on here. This country has suffered terribly at the hands of the political elites and those that do their bidding. I must also add the US State Department has publicly stated that Haiti is a source, transit and destination for men, women and children subjected to forced labour and trafficking and that the Government of Haiti does not fully meet the minimum standard for the elimination of trafficking. However it is making significant efforts to do so. I'll defer to Daniel now, as he's at the coal face so to speak."

"Bonjour et byen venu, don't worry, I will now speak in English. It's good that you are here, however, it is my job to warn you that my country is a very dangerous place and I have grave misgivings with your intentions, however if you do decide to go ahead, I will do my best to help. I must stress that we keep this here in this room and between ourselves. My department chief thinks I am here on routine security business, and with William's help my cover is secure. I am ashamed to admit that there are many here in Haiti who have benefited financially from the traffickers and their eyes and ears are everywhere."

I said a silent prayer of thanks and hoped my instinct to trust Daniel was well founded. It then turned to Raul to start asking key and important questions. My previous paranoia now distant in my memory.

"Daniel, we're going to need logistics on the main areas where the kids are taken to, any intel you have on the hubs that they're trafficked to. Has anyone managed to infiltrate or go undercover with these gangs?"

"I have brought with me today all the information we have and yes we tried to send in undercover agents, but their covers were blown and we found them with bullets to the back of the head, their eyes gouged out, their ears cut off and rags stuffed in their mouths. The warning was received loud and clear, hear nothing, say nothing, see nothing. My department never attempted it again, but we will never give up and with God's will and the help of people like you, we will and must win."

Raul didn't bat an eyelid or display any outward emotion at that last snippet of information, but then no doubt he'd seen much worse in his Navy Seal days. He was in reconnaissance mode and it was impressive to witness. It filled me with a renewed sense of energy and faith, knowing that we were in such strong, safe and indomitable hands.

Daniel informed us that the main hub for the trafficked children was in the northeast region of Haiti and to the west region of the Dominican Republic where there are unofficial crossing points at Ferrier and Capotille close to the official crossing point of Ouanaminthe.

This area is used to traffic children into the Dominican Republic, many of whom are used in the sex trade in several locations, Cabarete, Porto Plato and Sosua for example where mainly western men can indulge in their paedophilic predilections, free from the laws that would see them behind bars in their home countries.

Other information Daniel shared left us all visibly shocked. He was disseminating details that were implicating western humanitarian aid workers as big participants in the sex trade, the very people who were supposed to be saving the victims of the run of natural disasters that had befallen Haiti. I had read about this during my research but to have it confirmed by someone who had first-hand knowledge, brought it home all over again.

He also relayed the case of a former special agent with the US Department of Homeland Security who had located where many trafficked children were being held before transit to the Dominican Republic, it was in the hills of Petion-Ville, so another place of interest for us. He also imparted information that I was already aware of through my research concerning a woman called Lauren Silcott.

This woman came to Haiti with missionaries from several children's charities, all based out of the US, shortly after the devastating earthquake in 2010, and was arrested at the border trying to take thirty-three "orphans" from the devastated town of Calabrese and the slum of Le Citron out of Haiti to the Dominican Republic.

Fortunately a keen-eyed police officer noticed they did not have the proper authorisation for transporting the children across the border and they were all arrested including Silcott.

A former US president in one of his first acts as special envoy for the UN personally intervened on Silcott's behalf and by the time of the trial the charges had been reduced to 'arranging irregular travel'.

Silcott had also previously attempted to take a group of forty children, but police officers acting on a tip off turned her back at the border. What made this seem even more insidious is that not one of the children were orphans. Add to this the first attorney engaged by Silcott, a guy called Pablo Estevez was himself later arrested in connection with an international smuggling ring and accused of trafficking women and minors from Central America and Haiti.

All this was largely ignored by the western media, but that in itself only served to fuel my growing suspicions at what had been going on for so long with the children of Haiti and my heart was breaking all over again.

The next piece of information led me to look at Christian and he gave me the slightest of nods in acknowledgement of my stare.

Daniel told of other exit points from Haiti used by the traffickers, in the west and south of the island, the areas which were surrounded by the Caribbean Sea.

The intelligence reports covering this transit hub suggested that abducted children were taken by boat to several privately owned islands. These islands are owned by billionaires, they are playgrounds for themselves and their 'elite' guests.

The hairs on the back of my neck started to rise as I recalled Christian telling me of Candace's family owning an island in the Caribbean, what were the odds?

Now my imagination was indeed running away with me. I made a mental note to ask Christian the location of Candace's private family island once the meeting was over and it was just the two of us together.

Daniel then gave us another revelation, one which just made my heart sink lower. He told us that not only were there children being trafficked from Haiti into the Dominican Republic and beyond, but there was intelligence to back up chatter that the same was happening via an island just off Port au Prince bay called Gonave Island, just thirty-seven miles away.

Pathetically poor, Gonave Island had also been ravaged by the earthquake in 2010. It looked almost certain that children were being taken by boat firstly to the largest settlement of Anse a Galets, held there before being smuggled along to the fishing village of Latanye and trafficked out of there.

So not only were we going to investigate the crossings from Haiti into the Dominican Republic it was looking increasingly likely that we should also add Gonave Island to our areas of interest.

The next few hours were spent working on a watertight plan.

It became clearer why the fabrication of me being an archaeologist had been used in my false papers and that of the one for Christian too.

Archaeological digs have been rare in Haiti because of its political and civil instability, but for several years now it has been opening up and allowing many archaeological expeditions to take place.

Our cover was going to be that we were involved in working on a palace called Sans-Souci and an enormous fort called the Citadel. These structures covered a colourful part of Haiti's history and in particular a man called Henry Christophe who formed a kingdom in the north of the country, which worked well for our cover, as one of the main areas of interest to us was in the North. Sans-Souci was erected in the village of Milot, ten miles south of the northern port of Le Cap.

I found myself becoming increasingly more comfortable with Daniel, Christian and Raul appeared the same too. He was passionate about stopping the trafficking which was blighting his country and all the heinous cruelty that went hand in hand with human trafficking.

More than once he thanked us for being there for his country and its vulnerable children, he had started to become jaded and frustrated with the whole rescue effort being appropriated by celebrities, who once the cameras stopped clicking disappeared into the ether. Or the billions of dollars raised by charities that never reached its intended causes.

By 3 p.m., we were all feeling pretty drained but had covered so much. We all agreed that a break was needed so Christian, Raul and I would return to the guest house, grab a few hours' sleep, I could phone home and we would all meet for dinner at 8p.m..

Chapter 12

The mood and conversation during the short trip in the SUV from the embassy to the guest house was upbeat and quite positive, it really did feel that we were forming a strong team.

Raul however cautioned against being too confident, that we were entering an arena of undoubted danger, where the players were incredibly ruthless and were without a shred of conscience or humanity.

That they would kill in the blink of an eye anybody who threatened their sick multi-billion-dollar industry.

He added those responsible for human trafficking were no different to the South American drug cartels in their utter and total ruthlessness.

He echoed my thoughts on the team being strong and emphasised he knew we were all going in with our eyes wide open to the risks. With the ultimate goal of possibly rescuing these children being worth it a thousand times over.

Arriving at the guest house and as luck would have it, Raul bade us farewell quickly, claiming he was keen to return to his room and get his head down for a few hours.

Perfect timing for me to have Christian on his own and bring up the private island statement made by Daniel. I was far too keyed up to beat about the bush and just came straight out with it as we walked back to our rooms.

"What did you make of Daniel's comments on the trafficking of children to the private islands because what are the chances of you mentioning out of the blue only a couple of weeks ago that your in-laws just happen to own one, and you and I discussing that during my research I'd read that children were being trafficked to these islands and now there's corroborated intelligence that children are indeed being taken to these places for God knows what reasons."

"Hell Julia, I don't know if there's a connection, and it's a fucking big leap without evidence. I only mentioned as a statement of fact that Candace's parents own one, granted I also told you that there I'd been witness to some pretty strange stuff, like Masonic crap, but dodgy handshakes and outfits doesn't make them child traffickers or worse, does it?"

"Hey, I'm not saying it does, so let's agree to keep an open mind on everything that is going to be thrown our way in the next few weeks, as I have a very strong and indefatigable feeling that our worlds are going to be turned upside down. That we are all going to have to confront the very real possibility that people or institutions we have believed in most of our lives are just corrupt and evil."

"I don't doubt it Julia, but for now I'm going to try and grab some sleep and get my head around what we found out today. See you in the foyer at 8 p.m." With that he abruptly shut down further discussion and opened his room door, entering before quickly closing the door behind him.

Chastened by his somewhat curt reply I walked the short distance to my room.

I showered and before that much needed nap I called home. I used the guest house phone as Raul had insisted I no longer use my own mobile. That at some point burner phones would be arranged, it did indeed feel like I was in an episode of C.S.I. Raul was covering every base, every facet, nothing was being left to chance.

Steve had just arrived home from walking the dog and sounded tired as with the time difference it was late, giving me the perfect excuse to keep the call brief. At least I'd made contact and he knew I was OK.

After the long meeting at the embassy the last thing I needed was an interrogation and anyway we'd all agreed that what was discussed in that conference room stayed there or at least stayed between the five of us.

I pulled down the blinds, leaving the windows open as the warm breeze was welcome, laid down on the bed and began to drift off almost immediately.

It didn't take long before the first faces and voices began to appear to me. They were talking all at once which was confusing my exhausted and sleepy brain.

Above the cacophony of little ones' voices I could make out several words, afraid I'd break the link I memorised the eight words I was hearing repeatedly and just let the faces wash over me in a wave.

Sleep must have come soon after the last face disappeared from my view and I woke to my trusted old travel alarm clock announcing it was 7 p.m.

Feeling a little drowsy, it took me several moments to come to and remembering the eight words I'd memorised in the twilight zone, I clambered across the bed for my backpack and retrieved my Haitian Creole to English dictionary.

I replayed what the voices were saying to me in my mind whilst flipping through the dictionary, those eight words going round and round in my head. I prayed I'd remembered them correctly.

My fingers working quickly to locate the relevant pages, scribbling the translated words down onto my notepad. Sitting back to read the written sentence, "Manman ou se isit pou konseve pou yo," in English it read "Mother you are here to save them."

The tears started, the little ones were here with me, why was I surprised? It wouldn't matter what country I was in would it, they hardly needed an aeroplane to reach me! I felt enveloped by a feeling of inner peace, and calm, that we were on the right track had been confirmed by their visit and message.

Having showered and dressed I made my way along to the foyer where Christian and Raul were already waiting for me. Within a minute I noticed headlights, Christian grabbed my arm and ushered me towards the vehicle pulling up in front of the guest house.

As the uniformed driver exited the minibus the interior light came on and I could see that William, Daniel and a third person were seated in the vehicle.

Once Christian, Raul and I were seated William introduced us to the unknown man. His name was David Hearst, he nodded to the three of us, his role wasn't revealed until we were seated in the restaurant of the hotel William had arranged for us to eat in. He joked that we weren't to worry as it was a C.I.A. friendly place, somehow I didn't think he was joking.

David Hearst it transpired was an undercover agent who specialised in drug and human trafficking, he had been seconded to the US embassy in Port au Prince for six months and had been involved in some pretty impressive drugs busts in South America with links to human trafficking rings.

These two heinous activities it seems often went hand in hand, an 'industry' which spans the globe and was truly sickening in its enormity. He had also spent some time in Puerto Rico, and although this island had come up during my research, there didn't appear to be much mention of its connection to human trafficking.

Sadly it was becoming abundantly clear that most of the islands in this hemisphere were in some way linked to this vile trade.

Alas I still had the nagging doubt that too many people were becoming involved, it just wouldn't go away. Deep in my gut the worry that I didn't know who to trust, perhaps my mind was just working overtime due to the depth of such dreadful information I had filled my head with recently.

Where with just a few clicks on a search engine anyone could discover the very real fact that presidents, top government officials, civil servants, aid organisations and aid workers, the very people in society we are supposed to trust were deeply implicated in aiding and abetting the felons. All the while reaping enormous financial rewards for their complicity and silence.

I simply had to put these feelings to one side, to snap out of my current wayward thinking. In short, place my trust in these people.

Chapter 13

Upon entering the restaurant we were ushered into a private dining room. I headed straight for the table, followed by Christian and Raul. Good they were taking a seat on either side of me.

I already felt immensely comfortable and at ease in Raul's company, we had connected instantly, bonded even. It helped too that I also felt safer with him around us.

Glancing around the table I took note of William and David talking quietly to each other, Christian picked up on it too, they noticed us and William casually informed the table of David's concern for privacy.

William stated matter-of-fact that the room had been 'swept' for listening devices. It seemed I was the only one surprised at this declaration, in my somewhat limited experience I'd only heard of such things in spy thriller movies, my naivety was showing and big time.

As the first course of Bouillon was being served the table fell silent and that set a pattern for when each course was served. It became apparent not even waiters or waitresses were to be trusted.

The situation we were in was certainly hitting home big time, that trust in others outside of this room was to be kept to an absolute minimum if at all. That indeed this mission was being afforded the utmost security by consummate professionals in their fields of expertise. I started to relax for the first time since I'd left England.

Over the following courses of Griot, Accra Lambi Guisado and Lalo Legume, which Raul informed me were some of Haiti's national dishes, the genesis of a team began to take form.

The absolute last thing we needed was for this to be turned into a testosterone competition, but to my total and utter relief it appeared we all had one united goal. And that goal was to come hell or high water we'd try our damndest to rescue children from a terrifying fate.

From this night on I was to become Linda Grey, the archaeologist funded by an American university to explore and promote Haiti's rich history and heritage.

Christian's role was to be the representative of the University granting the funding and was accompanying me due to his knowledge of the region.

David and Raul's roles were to provide protection and security, sadly due to the violence and danger in Haiti this wouldn't raise any eyebrows.

Daniel's role was to be himself, as head of the Police force he would be personally ensuring that all artefacts found would remain the property of Haiti and not turn up at auction houses and into the hands of collectors whose morals were questionable. As he was well known for his knowledge and passion for archaeology, his addition to the team would be deemed feasible to any that questioned it.

Huge efforts were being made in attempting to keep this under the radar and non-political, it was a good call. The very last thing needed was for the US to be linked in any way to foreign nationals working undercover.

By the end of dinner we were pretty much up to speed with everything. We would be leaving the following evening, much better to travel in darkness, it would attract less attention.

William and Daniel had already organised our transport. They had arranged two vehicles, one a truck big enough to transport all the 'archaeological' equipment, food, water and camping gear, the second a SUV for us to travel in slightly more comfort.

All our documentation was in order should we be stopped, and licenses granting permission to carry out archaeological works sanctioned. We were as ready as we ever would be to embark on a journey that was fraught with danger and the unknown.

We said our goodbyes and Raul took Christian and I back to the guest house. On the short journey we were all quiet and contemplative, each lost in our own thoughts. Mine on the enormity of what we were undertaking, reality hitting me that I had three beautiful children thousands of miles away who had absolutely no idea what their Mum was doing.

A husband who did know and who was far from happy with it. A maelstrom of emotions was tearing through me, but it was far too late now to have second thoughts, this was all happening because of me.

I'd come this far and with the aid of some pretty incredible people, who in such a short space of time had not only believed in me but had put together a plan that could very well set them in harm's way without once questioning my claims of children being in mortal peril.

As I was opening the door to my room I heard approaching footsteps, it was Christian carrying what looked like a bottle of Kentucky's finest, a bucket of ice and two glasses, any notion of an early night quickly evaporated.

"I thought we could do with going over a few points that weren't covered at dinner, and I'm too wired to sleep."

"Well I guess you'd better come in then, this is taking me back to our university days when you first introduced me to bourbon, Steve still blames you for my taste for it."

Once inside, Christian proceeded to fix the drinks and settle down on the only chair in the room, I took the bed and waited for him to start the conversation, which he did without preamble.

"I don't want you to worry any more than I know you are right now, but William has arranged for us to be armed for the trip, you know your way around guns but I needed to warn you beforehand."

"Frankly, Christian, I feel better knowing we will have that protection, but I assumed it would be just Raul, David and Daniel that would be authorised to carry firearms."

"Julia, there's nothing about this trip that is authorised, William is really going out on a limb with this, ditto Daniel and Raul. William could face a whole shit storm for what he's doing, instigating an unsanctioned investigation into a foreign country being the tip of the iceberg, in fact I was more than a little surprised at his readiness to go all in on this. I genuinely thought he would help, but to the extent that he has, has astounded me."

"Yes, I can see that, but surely any human being with an ounce of compassion, empathy et al and who had the means and power to help, would. Although granted he is putting his whole career and standing on the line for what could be a wild goose chase, on the whim of a middle-aged English woman who channels dead children. I have to ask though, do you trust William implicitly?"

"Hey, do not speak like that, these guys know what's been going on. They are fully aware of the depth of depravity involved. But human trafficking has been going on for a long time with enough people in high places to cover it up, maybe it's time for good to conquer at least some of the evil in this world. As for trusting William, well I don't think we have a choice."

Christian was correct we really didn't have a choice and William had really smoothed our way so far. This made me feel so much better and positive. Especially the good conquering evil part.

I would replay that sentence over in my mind many times in the forthcoming days, to bolster my resolve and faith.

By the time we'd almost finished the bottle, Christian reminded me of David's request over dinner that we leave our cell phones, laptops, passports and any jewellery for safekeeping at the Embassy whilst we were in the 'field'.

Reiterating David and Daniel would both be issued with satellite phones, that they would be our only form of communication for the entire trip. He double checked that my inoculations for hepatitis and cholera were up to date. It seemed like we had dotted the I's and crossed all the T's for the time being anyway. I then had to admit I was dog tired and needed some sleep, fortunately Christian concurred.

As I walked him to the door he turned and planted a kiss on my lips that seemed to linger a tad longer than I felt comfortable with, must be the bourbon I thought as he left the room.

Chapter 14

I awoke early, with just a trace of a headache to a very wet and humid morning, was it the bourbon or the impending storm, both I surmised.

Regardless I had several things I needed to do, the first being writing emails to Lucy, Jacob and Ethan, I'd already worked out in my head what I would write. That we were heading off to a region with little or no wireless reception, so contact would be nigh on impossible, they weren't to worry as Uncle Christian was with me along with other journalists. It was quite a good group and we were all rather excited.

I hated lying, it went against everything I stood for. Indeed I had never lied to my children before apart from Father Christmas and the tooth fairy, those wonderful, innocent elements of childhood. I reasoned with myself that it was kinder this way, they'd only worry with knowing the truth.

One down with one to go. I emailed Steve, I took the cowards way out as I really couldn't bear to hear the rapprochement in his voice over the telephone. Much easier to just write a few words and press send.

With emails sent, I texted Christian about breakfast, the bourbon had left me with an acid stomach and I needed to eat. He replied almost immediately that he'd ordered a cab to arrive in forty minutes to take us to a restaurant called La Fouchet.

It wasn't far, situated on the Boulevard du 15 Octobre, but I was beginning to realise that strolling around Port Au Prince wasn't really advisable. At least I had forty minutes to shower and wash my hair, I didn't know when I'd next be able to so I stood under the shower for a while, savouring every minute.

I was dressed and ready to go when I heard the knock on the door, Christian can only be described as anal in his punctuality and there he was, looking as eager to eat as me. On the cab ride to the La Fouchet, Christian mentioned that it was William who had recommended the place, being a favourite for embassy staff as it had American style breakfasts on the menu. As long as that didn't include grits I'd be fine. Strong coffee and biscuits would be just what I needed and it didn't disappoint.

"Fill your boots Julia because God knows what we'll get to eat once we leave the city, whatever Raul and William are organising I think it's all going to come in a can."

"I'm of the opinion that food will be well down our list of priorities my darling, frankly I don't care if it's beans and water, I just so desperately want to get going now." I didn't add that I'd had the voices again last night, this time it was "Fe vit, Fe vit Fe vit" which I'd translated as "hurry, hurry, hurry."

Just for a short while it felt like old times, two friends having breakfast on a shaded terrace, enjoying each other's' company and the surroundings basked in warm sunshine. When I mentioned this to Christian, his beautiful smile acknowledged his agreement.

"We've certainly had some adventures during our friendship Julia, so many wonderful memories. I thank God often for the serendipity of our first ever meeting. You know sometimes it only feels like yesterday, man I'm beginning to sound like my dad."

I had to giggle at that. "I know exactly what you mean on both counts. I often sit and reminisce and I can recall so much like it was only yesterday. As for sounding like my mum, I think it's more Clara that I sound like. As you know well, we had such an incredible bond, I feel her around me so much, it's almost tangible, that I could reach out and actually touch her. And no, I'm not going cranky if that's what you're thinking, she started me on this journey, without her 'gift' passed down to me, all of this would never be happening. So many strange things have happened to me, I used to think it was just fate playing its hand, but as I've grown older, I truly believe other forces have been at play."

"One day when all this is over, will you tell me everything Julia, and I mean everything, lock, stock and barrel. I've a feeling you have held back so much from everybody including Steve."

"I promise I will, but you are going to have to open your academic mind to the very real possibility that not every answer to life's questions can be answered in black and white."

"I'll raise a glass to that and promise to keep an open mind, and on that note let's make our way back, as I have a few emails I need to send before we go dark."

Christian had paid the taxi driver to wait for us whilst we ate, so luckily we didn't have to hang around, and we were back at our accommodation in just a few minutes. We were being picked up at 6 p.m., so as I was already packed I had time to read the archaeological information I'd been given, just in case I was questioned about my presence in Haiti, to try and give it a veneer of authenticity. It was pretty in depth and there was no way I'd finish it by 6 p.m., I decided I'd stash it in my backpack and finish it later.

Dead on the nail of 6 p.m. the black SUV pulled into the forecourt, we loaded our luggage and headed for the Embassy. Once we arrived, we were led to the same room we'd had the first meeting in.

The others were all there waiting for us. Without fanfare William produced what looked like safety deposit boxes for our mobile phones and jewellery, although I insisted on keeping my wedding band, that had never been off my finger, since the day all those years ago I'd taken my vows with Steve.

Then cases for our laptops, our suitcases would be put in storage too. I'd packed the basics, change of clothes and toiletries in my backpack, we were definitely travelling light. Thank God for converse, one pair fits all requirements for where we were heading.

We were then taken to a courtyard within the Embassy grounds where a uniformed man produced the guns we were being issued with, M9 berettas.

Although I'd been around and familiar with guns all my life, this particular type was new to me. The guy in uniform informed us it was standard military issue, and proceeded to demonstrate loading and reloading.

He passed one each to Christian and I, asked us to perform the loading and reloading, then pointed to the target practice and instructed us to "get familiar with the firearm."

Christian's effort was perfect, five shots, three to the head and two to the chest. I was definitely rusty and mine sailed past the target, much to my embarrassment, however I calmly reloaded and managed four out of five, each shot hitting the torso. With a "that's not bad Ma'am," he nodded to William and left us.

"William is this necessary?" I had to ask the question, obviously I was aware that human traffickers were dangerous people, but I thought it would be enough with just the guys being armed.

"Julia, my mantra has always been, better to be safe than sorry and from all the intelligence reports these bastards are well armed. Where there are big bucks involved, you can rest assured guns will naturally follow. And anyways Christian told me that you grew up around a farm and are comfortable with firearms."

"Most of that is true, but I wouldn't say I was comfortable, it just came with the territory, you know a farming family. Controlling foxes and clay pigeon shooting is a world away from a beretta and can these be traced back to the Embassy if we are stopped and searched?"

"Don't worry about that Julia, there are no loose ends."

Christian piped in "I wouldn't expect anything else my friend, what you are doing here is nothing short of incredible. I know I speak for Julia too, without you we wouldn't be anywhere near as prepared and protected."

"Well just promise me to both come back in one piece. I've got to admit initially I thought you'd lost the plot. Don't get me wrong we've known for a long-time trafficking is big business here and others have tried to do something before with limited success, but there's a new sheriff in town now."

I immediately realised what William was referring to "Do you mean the executive order issued in December 2017, blocking the property of people involved in serious human rights or corruption, does that cover Human trafficking?"

"Yes and a task force has been set up, inter agency so all the right people are talking to each other, which believe me helps, after years of procrastination, deliberate or otherwise, eradicating human trafficking is now high on the agenda."

Christian chimed in with "amen to that."

William then led us back inside the Embassy, we now only had a couple of hours before we were due to depart, and I was amazed at how calm I actually felt now.

A small buffet had been laid out in our absence and the others had waited for us to return, before eating. I stood slightly back from the others', wanting to take the time to observe each of my fellow travellers in turn.

Raul, so desperate to make his beloved Haiti safe and good again, Daniel, so passionate about ending the agony of human trafficking, David, so eager to help us with his vast knowledge of trafficking gangs and finally my dearest friend Christian, who had taken a whole leap of faith in believing me from the word go.

Lastly, William Monroe, a man who I'd only known a few short days, and yet who had moved heaven and earth to make this a reality.

I said a silent prayer of thanks to my God and the men in this room. Swiftly followed by a prayer to keep us safe and our mission a success.

Chapter 15
The Journey

Psalm 91:11 For he will command his angels concerning you, to guard you in all your ways.

It was nearing 10 p.m. when we headed out to the awaiting vehicles. Christian and I were to travel in the SUV with Daniel driving, whilst Raul and David were taking the truck. As Christian wanted to sit up front with Daniel, I went to take the back seat, as I did so William approached me, and what seemed most out of character, hugged me and whispered in my ear "Go save the kids and tell them I'm sorry Julia." The lump in my throat and tears in my eyes were immediate. Although the last part of his sentence seemed odd, why would he be sorry? All I could muster in response was a nod and a peck on his cheek. With that we were off into the night.

We had decided to take the route north east to the area around Ouanaminthe, which in theory would take us approximately five hours, right through the interior of Haiti.

Our other option was to take a more direct route via Route National 3, but the decision was made to take a more circuitous route, hopefully drawing less attention to ourselves, especially as we ran the risk of being seen leaving the embassy and who was I to argue.

There was little point in trying to take in the surroundings as it was dark. The night a pitch-black curtain that seemed to cocoon us inside the SUV, lending an ethereal air, punctuated by a myriad of stars, battling for room on the great tableau of the sky at night. So, I just made myself comfortable, I was about to put my ear buds in when Daniel struck up a conversation.

"Did you know that in Haitian folklore there is a figure called 'Uncle Knapsack', the folktales say he abducted children, we Haitians are a very superstitious race and I believe that many of my countrymen and women still think that it is he who is responsible for all the missing children, I sometimes think some myths have been perpetuated to cover for what we know has been going on. The Tontons Macoutes took their name from him, the henchmen of Duvalier. We have had many dark periods in our nation's history, and Papa Doc was responsible for perhaps the worst."

I replied, "Yes indeed, Daniel, your country has suffered so much through its history, sadly most people are totally unaware of it and I hope you don't mind me saying, but only associate Haiti with voodoo and zombies, more myths perpetuated, though this time mostly by Hollywood."

Daniel continued, "So very true, but I'm sure you have read the real meaning of the Zombie, which is how we refer to it in creole. As for the vodou, well you are correct in what you say, it is a religion, far removed from the Hollywood depiction of it. Brought over from West and Central Africa with the slaves, Haitian Vodou is unique to Haiti and was birthed in the plantations those poor souls were indentured to. They only had their religion, but the French who shipped them here were afraid of it and made them convert to Catholicism, but they found ways to keep it alive and even intertwined them both, that's why if you visit a Vodou temple you will often find catholic images too."

Christian joined the conversation. "When all this is over I would very much like to explore your country Daniel, it is unique in so many ways and so beautiful."

The genuine warmth in Daniel's voice was apparent as he added, "I would consider it an honour to be your guide Christian, and you too Julia, perhaps in some small way it will be my way of thanking you both from the bottom of my heart for what you have set in motion to help the children of my country."

The conversation flowed, as I began to feel weary and my eyelids were becoming heavier. I must have dropped off to sleep as the next thing I noticed was that the SUV had stopped, my door was opened and Christian was gently nudging me awake. "Wake up sleepy head, time for a comfort break and coffee."

We had stopped just outside of a place called Thomonde, which is situated in the Central Plateau of Haiti and is part of the Hinche Arrondissement according to Raul, who insisted on giving us a geography lesson whilst preparing coffee.

Apparently, we'd made good time, as the roads were dry, making them much more accessible and our path so far unhindered.

I wandered off to pee behind the nearest tree, when I returned the guys were hunched over a map splayed out on the bonnet of the SUV, Raul torch in hand was examining it intently. They concurred between themselves to carry on to Hinche, from there we'd take the road to Thomassque onto Cerca la Source, then onto Ouanaminthe, as they were sure we weren't being followed, we could travel the rest of our journey on relatively good roads.

Back on the road again, filled to the brim with caffeine, there was no way on earth I'd sleep the rest of the way. It seemed it'd had the same effect on Christian too, so he took the opportunity to grill me on all things archaeological, I guessed he'd been reading up too. Daniel was very knowledgeable, adding much needed facts to my rapidly growing erudition of all things archaeological and historical relating to Haiti, she was indeed a country rich in both.

We arrived at our destination just after 2.30 a.m., With the headlights of both vehicles illuminating our locale, I could see the rough track we'd taken had brought us to a clearing in a wooded area and in front of us were several quite dilapidated buildings.

Raul explained briefly that this once would have been a Lakou, a small village and luckily this one had been built with corrugated-iron roofs and not thatched, so although in bad repair, the roofs were still relatively in good order and would afford us some protection. The isolated spot would also not draw attention to us.

David added that they had monitored satellite imagery for the area and there had been no movement in or around it for quite a while. This I found pretty impressive and William's comment of "we've covered everything" sprung to mind.

This would be our base, although tents had been brought with us for any forays into unpopulated areas, we also hadn't ruled out using guest houses too, to give a less secretive air to the expedition. Hiding in plain sight was the term Daniel had used.

We all helped to unload our sleeping bags from the truck, apart from David who busied himself with setting up the camping gas stove to heat water for coffee. I was thankful for the American adoration of coffee, no matter where you were, a pot of coffee would always seem to appear. Just like on the many camping trips my family and I had taken with Christian.

I felt a sudden and painful pang of guilt, for my family thousands of miles away totally unaware, apart from Steve, what I was entering into. I said to myself quickly that they would understand, of course they would, they were used to my many crusades for what I believed were good and deserving causes, and this certainly usurped all of the previous ones.

With torchlights in hand, we went to inspect the buildings, as expected they had some detritus in them, but nothing too bad, apart from some enormous spider webs and that is my Achilles heel, I am terrified of spiders.

I always have been since early childhood. Knowing me well, Christian grabbed a long piece of wood and gallantly tried to clear most of them, managing some humour as he took a bow after his efforts.

Still not convinced that it was arachnid free, I rolled out my sleeping bag in the middle of the room, then searched through my rucksack for my trusted bug spray, and proceeded to cover myself in it.

The sleeping arrangements were to be the same as our travel teams, Christian, Daniel and & I together, whilst Raul and David would take the most habitable one nearest ours.

Raul, David and Daniel agreed to take turns in staying awake, keeping a lookout for any unwanted visitors. Relieved I wasn't included in sentry duty I climbed into my sleeping bag, not even bothering to take off my trusted converse, the less areas exposed to arachnids friendly or otherwise being my raison d'etre.

Finding sleep difficult with so many thoughts flying around inside my head, I eventually began to relax enough to drift off. I wasn't aware how long I'd been in the twilight zone, only that when I felt myself being urged to wake up by Christian, the voices became more insistent and urgent. They were desperate for the link not to be broken before the message was relayed to me.

I came to as Daniel was kneeling beside me, torchlight in hand. "Julia, you were speaking in Creole repeating over and over "Manman prese, Manman prese, Manman prese," what is going on here?"

By the time I was fully awake Christian had fired up the camping light, casting the room in eerie shadow, which only added to my heightened sense of panic and alarm.

It took several minutes for me to calm down and my heart rate to lower. By this time Raul and David had joined us. David on sentry duty had, upon seeing the light come on, and hearing our voices, roused Raul assuming there might be a problem.

I looked askance at Christian, and he nodded. We'd agreed with William to omit any reference to my conduit abilities with Daniel and David, and Raul was already privy to this information from our initial meeting. Sticking to a joint agreement that it was my research that had led me to Haiti.

With Christian's tacit approval I sat up and started to try and explain to the men gathered around me my nightly visits from the realm of spirit.

"Firstly, you must understand that we have never set out to mislead you guys, we were so very concerned you'd think I was a crank and dismiss it immediately. You see I have a spiritual gift that was passed down to me from my paternal Grandmother Clara. It took a while for Christian to wrap his head around it, but our deep friendship meant he knew I'd never lie or fabricate anything to him." The look on their collective faces was one of polite incredulity.

So I continued on, relaying basically what I'd told Christian, Raul, and later William. Emphasising that up until recent events the children had only appeared as faces, fleeting images, exactly what Clara had experienced.

However, suddenly this had rapidly changed. That the silent faces were no longer fleeting images and they were actually voicing, no begging me to help them.

That it was this that had led me to research Haiti in particular as I'd recited their pleas over and over in my head until I'd discovered they were speaking Haitian Creole to me. And when I interpreted their pleas, I began to piece together what these poor souls were asking of me.

The first to start speaking to me was Daniel, "I was raised a catholic, but my grandmothers' practised Vodou, both of which believe in the spirit world do they not, one is the Holy Spirit and the other Iwa. I also believe in a higher force, one that cannot be explained, from which miracles can occur and Julia I think your gift is a miracle sent from God to help these poor souls and for that I thank you."

Completely taken aback by Daniel's candour and as tears sprang to my eyes, I reached over to him with my arms outspread and just hugged him tightly. "Thank you, Daniel, your words mean so much to me".

Raul was the next to articulate his feelings "I have learned through life, that there are many strange things that I cannot understand, nor possess the awareness to question. I do however fully believe in divine serendipity, in that I feel God has brought us together in this quest, how else can we explain two journalists, a diplomat, a police chief, an undercover agent and of course myself, being brought together."

That left David. "I don't mind admitting that I have never believed in either God or any other religion and I'm having trouble believing what I'm hearing. I deal in black and white, it's the only way I've kept myself sane with what I have to deal with in my line of work. So I'll ask for time to think through this, but I will add that I'm beginning to think there's something to this 'God works in mysterious ways' gumbo, how else can we explain us here now, So perhaps Raul has a point.".

Christian reacted by saying "I think I can speak on behalf of Daniel, Julia and Raul, that we can live with that David, as we all have the same goal here."

By now the sun was beginning to rise, after the blackness of the night I welcomed it. I went to sit on what passed for a doorstep and drank in the colours appearing before me, the sky filling with shades of orange and pink, peach and magenta, nature at its finest and most beautiful.

A new day was dawning and I couldn't help but wonder what this day would bring. I found myself involuntarily rubbing my hand on the wooden door frame, it was one of Clara's idiosyncrasies, "just for luck dear" she would say.

I smiled inwardly at the recollection, and felt the all too familiar warm glow that encompassed me whenever I thought of my dearest Nan. I know you're with me Clara, I thought to myself. I can feel you all around me, you're my talisman.

I said a silent prayer for her to help guide us and to keep us all safe.

Chapter 16

Psalm 23:4 Even I walk through the darkest valley, I will fear no evil, for you are with me; your rod and your staff, they comfort me.

After Raul had fed us a very tasty and typical Haitian breakfast of fried plantains and eggs, I excused myself to go get changed and thankfully clean my teeth, wash my face and generally tidy myself up in preparation for the day ahead.

As I did so I reflected on the beautiful morning, thankfully still dry, so the roads would be accessible and the sky a clear blue aquamarine without the hint of a cloud to be seen, perfect conditions for our expedition.

As we busied ourselves rolling up our sleeping bags and loading everything onto the truck in readiness for our departure, the birds were entertaining us with a symphony of song, welcoming the day as only our feathered friends can, it was a joy to listen to them.

But all too soon Daniel gave us the signal to head off. Keeping the same seating arrangements as the overnight journey, and with that we were on our way.

We were roughly skirting the border with the Dominican Republic, although some miles back, between Ouanaminthe and Fort Liberte.

Fortunately, there are plenty of archaeological sites to the north, giving us the perfect cover should our presence be called into question.

I made a mental note that I was now Linda Grey, I needed to become accustomed with my new persona and almost as if he were reading my mind Christian reminded me.

"We have to start calling you Linda from here on in, have you memorised your new date of birth etc?"

"Crikey, that is spooky as I was just thinking about it and yes I've memorised everything, down to the last detail."

"Excellent, we can't be too careful, loose lips sinks ships and all that."

"Absolutely right," added Daniel.

For the next few miles we travelled in silence, I was keen to take in my surroundings, as we'd only travelled in darkness since our arrival. It was like travelling back in time, as it is in so many of the Caribbean islands.

My eyes drank in the sights along our way. From brightly coloured clapper board houses, though many were rundown and in need of repair, to the land farmed in terraces and an abundance of banana trees, and in the distance I could just make out the mountains with rings of cloud covering the highest peaks.

Haiti is without doubt a beautiful country I thought to myself. An intrepid explorer's paradise awaited those with the foresight to grab it with both hands.

Taking the route around Ouanaminthe and heading straight to Fort Liberte had been agreed before we set out as David had good intel that the area around the border at Dajabon had attracted too much attention from the authorities for the traffickers to use this route into the Dominican Republic any longer.

There was also growing evidence that the Dominican Republic was being bypassed altogether, that "the merchandise" was being shipped from the coast between Fort Liberte and Cap Haitien by sea in several directions, depending on the final destination for the cargo.

"Cargo or merchandise" such a sick adjective for human lives, it made me sick to my stomach and incensed to hear these descriptions and only served to strengthen my resolve and extinguish totally any doubts as to why we were here.

With the up-to-date intel that David was privy to, we stood a fighting chance at locating the new hubs and exposing them, not before rescuing as many children as we were possibly capable of.

It all seemed so simple and plausible when I played it out in my mind.

Once exposed for the world to see, this could not be covered up any longer. The corrupt would not be protected or able to protect the gangs, they would have no place to hide or illicit dollars to fund them.

Haiti would be free at last to heal and perhaps take its deserved place as a safe destination for travel, and reap the rewards of much needed tourism.

My musings were interrupted by David announcing we were nearing Fort Liberte. We were going to make a planned stop here, ostensibly to pick up supplies but also to meet with a contact of his.

At the entrance to the town Daniel pointed out a bright yellow arch and informed us this was called the "Belle entrée" and that we would park up near Place D'Armes.

We managed to park near the Cathedral and regrouped, with David leading the way to a small parade of buildings with awnings out front. One had several tables and chairs set outside, it was a little restaurant cum coffee house.

Somewhat deserted as it was still quite early, that being apart from a solitary gentleman sat at one of the tables, clothed in a white linen suit.

He immediately gave me the impression of the quintessential Englishman abroad. I wasn't wrong in my assumption.

As we approached the table he stood up and doffed his Panama hat, revealing a shock of snowy white hair and greeted David with the air of two people who were well acquainted.

David introduced him as Robert Potter and in turn he shook hands with all of us.

After we were seated a young waitress appeared and Robert began a conversation with her in what I took to be French Creole, seeming at perfect ease with the language.

After she had retreated back inside the cafe door he proceeded to inform us he'd ordered coffees all round and he'd told her we were the archaeologists he was expecting to show around the forts that surrounded the bay, to also include a talk about the local flora and fauna.

With no one within earshot he carried on, albeit quietly,

"Welcome to Fort Liberte, I take it David has filled you in as to how I find myself in this backwater?"

We all looked rather non-plussed, obviously apart from David, who took this prompt to explain further.

"The guys only know we were to meet a contact of mine, I thought it best to leave the explaining to you Robert."

Robert had positioned himself in the chair that was directly opposite the door to the cafe, and kept an eye on it as he started to explain everything.

No doubt to change the subject once the waitress appeared with our beverages. Although quite how a young girl from a Haitian backwater would understand English I didn't know, then it dawned on me, Robert was obviously some sort of agent too and would be hyper alert to all things clandestine.

"Let me bring you up to speed. I am primarily a horticulturalist, an historian coming closely second. I've spent my adult life wandering this planet cataloguing rare and sometimes undocumented species of plants and succulents. During my travels to places such as the Yemen and Ethiopia to name but a few I gained the trust of many governmental officials, some rather dubious characters but useful nonetheless. Because you see, as a young man, the University I attended was a recruiting ground for MI5/MI6 and although I declined the offer then, preferring to gain my degree and experience in the field to build my reputation, I took up the offer later. You see it was the perfect ruse, a ruse that has served my country well. During my many years travelling the globe in my dual role I have been involved in many covert operations encompassing everything from terrorism to drug trafficking. But it was several years ago when I honestly considered it was about time to retire back to Blighty, that human trafficking appeared on my radar and of all the heinous activities I have covered, human trafficking has sickened me the most by far. So in a nutshell, I met David in Puerto Rico, we were introduced by our handlers and the rest they say is history."

I can confidently state that we were all collectively left somewhat speechless following Robert's introduction, however after an initial silence it was Daniel who took up the lead.

"That is without doubt one of the most incredible resumes I've ever heard Robert, it would appear that we have good company on our mission."

Robert continued "It's imperative that I add the principal reason for my being here in Haiti does involve horticulture, but on a medicinal front, you see there is a plant, indigenous to Haiti that is exciting the world of dementia research. It's extremely rare and bloody hard to find. The seeds of this plant are what is needed for the research, but David made contact knowing full well I'd want to be a part of what you're doing and I could also provide a good cover for whatever forays you go on. I have permits to search, locate and collect the seeds in all areas and over the months I've ingratiated myself well into the local communities. Hence the arousal of suspicion is exponentially lowered."

Robert rapidly changed the subject so I gathered as I had my back to the door, that the young waitress had returned, my assumption was correct and coffee was served. We continued chatting until we'd finished our drinks, Robert settled the tab and we were off to the nearby forts, the cover for our not so clandestine meeting.

It was only a ten minute walk or so and we arrived at Fort Dauphin. During the short walk Robert gave us a brief history lesson regarding the Fort, it had been built in 1731 to celebrate the birth of King Louis XV's son.

We walked along the thin spit of land and clambered up to the entrance, it appeared very overgrown and deserted so gave us a perfect spot away from prying eyes.

We made our way past the old barracks, along the ramparts to the end of the fort, Robert pointing out how, from this viewpoint we could understand the fort's strategic location in the bay. It was quite stunning and in turn sad, that such an historic landmark was in such a sad state of decay.

As we settled ourselves, I could see Robert and David were in a deep conversation, a little further away from the rest of us. After several minutes they joined us and Robert began to relay what they had been discussing.

"You have arrived at a crucial time, as there is a definite movement of children imminent. You see, when I sit in the corner of a bar nursing a rhum, apparently studying my research, I appear as an innocuous older man, and am paid little attention. But I listen to everything. Several evenings ago a group of men arrived at the bar, to be exact, two Americans, three Haitians and perhaps most intriguingly the head of a NGO working in the area. This chap has appeared in some communications I've received and hails from Bolivia. After their initial wariness had worn off, probably due to the copious amount of the local rhum they were imbibing, they were somewhat more relaxed and off guard and their lips shall we say were loosened. Once merchandise and cargo were mentioned, I listened intently, these arrogant bastards think no one is aware of the hidden connotations in their choice of descriptions. Suffice to say that as I previously mentioned, shipments are due and soon. Having heard enough, I bade them all "Bonnwit", best to leave before them, as it arouses less suspicion."

Raul, who had been very quiet since the cafe, began to question Robert. "Do you have any definite information of the transit locations?, as it would be like looking for a needle in a haystack, given the stretch of coastline and easy access to it."

Robert replied, "Good question Raul, yes we have some areas of interest, particularly around Cornier Plage and stretching further along the coast to Port-d-Paix where it is just a short boat ride to Ile de la Torture. Exit points are changed constantly in order to arouse less interest, please remember we are dealing with highly organised and extremely devious cartels, trafficking is big business and an extremely lucrative one to boot. I apologise in advance to both Raul and Daniel, although there are many now in officialdom here in Haiti who are determined to eradicate this heinous trade, there are still some in place who profit from it, be careful in whom you trust. In my experience sometimes it can be the person you least suspect."

Daniel interjected, "You do not tell us anything that we are not already aware of Robert, corruption runs deep, no country is free of it and when you have a country as poor as mine, the temptation is that much greater. However great strides are being made to root it out, many have used my country for their own personal piggy bank and abused its people in the process. The earthquake and its subsequent relief efforts bear testimony to this. There is much anger in Haiti and with that anger has grown a strong resolution for change for the better, that is why I am here and we will achieve it."

We all nodded our heads furiously in unison. Robert then produced an envelope that had been tucked into his trousers and hidden from view by his jacket, it contained copies of satellite imagery showing small convoys of vehicles which he explained were of suspected episodes of human trafficking. They included co-ordinates for these movements, which would hopefully assist us in narrowing down areas of interest, positive and most welcome information.

It did in fact appear that we were receiving help from the most unexpected sources and it felt so good and reassuring, the good guys working together.

Christian asked Robert if he would be accompanying us on the next leg of our reconnaissance, he wouldn't be joining us, explaining that it could possibly put his cover in jeopardy, and anyway he would be more use continuing the monitoring from a safe distance. He had a military satellite phone, as did we, so safe and untraceable contact would be no issue.

He then suggested we make our way back to the town, have lunch together at a little restaurant he was familiar with, he would then take us to a small market where we would be able to pick up some supplies. He seemed keen to introduce us to the locals as his archaeological friends', giving us good cover, as although the population was quite sparse, the "jungle wire" operated well.

After lunch and a walk into the local market, we bade Robert farewell, but I had the strongest feeling we would be seeing him again and soon. This enigmatic and utterly charming man had left rather a large impression on me, an impression of a humble yet brave and fiercely intelligent man. I also surmised that there was much, much more to him, that we had only been given a brief synopsis of his credentials, most definitely there were more bows in his quiver.

The afternoon was hot and humid, not one cloud had appeared in the pure blue sky and I was grateful for the air conditioning in the SUV, a most welcome respite from the heat.

Christian and Daniel were chatting up front as my eyelids became heavier, the early morning, the trek around the fort, lunch and trip to the market were catching up on me and I let myself succumb to a much needed siesta.

It was the bumpy road that woke me, I had no idea how long I'd been sleeping or where we were. I felt a little disoriented for just a minute or so, but turning in his seat and with a wink and a smile Christian welcomed me back to the world of the living and promptly informed me that we would be shortly arriving at our destination.

We'd followed the rocky archipelago, near the coast but needed forest for cover, so had come a little further inland.

We would pitch our tents here, a sort of base camp, not envisaging a short stay unless further intel led us otherwise or we struck lucky quickly, I was praying for the latter.

As we busied ourselves erecting the tents, I could hear running water, mentioning this to Raul, he took my arm and led me away from the camp clearing and into the wooded area.

After a short walk, the sound of cascading water became noticeably louder and then before us was the most enchanting natural pool of water, being fed by water tumbling down from a rocky outcrop.

My delight was written all over my face, and Raul smiling, too, as he told me this was not an uncommon sight in the forests of Haiti.

Taking the time to fully appreciate this marvel of nature, I noticed amongst all the greenery enveloping most of the rocks giving it an almost living facade, was what appeared to be a cave-like entrance.

"Oh Raul look, there's a cave entrance behind the waterfall," I was almost childlike in my wonderment and awe at this gem of nature. Little did I realise then the significant part this idyllic spot would end up playing later.

"You sound like a child who has discovered fairies at the bottom of your garden," Raul responded. "Daniel remembered this spot from his childhood and thought it a good place to stop, we can also minimise the use of the water we brought with us and bathe here, if necessary."

Now I thought of it, I hadn't showered since the guest house yesterday, the quick once over this morning hardly constituted a clean-up and I relished the idea of bathing here. It brought back memories of my holiday in Borneo, many years ago. Before the children had come along, Steve and I had started our trip in Kota Kinabalu, then travelled up to Sandakhan, "The Land Beneath the Wind", finally arriving at Sepilok, the orang-utan rescue centre. We'd totally embraced the jungle life which had included bathing in natural pools like this one. I couldn't resist it any longer, quickly pulling off my converse and socks, I sat on the bank and dipped my feet in the cool water, it was heavenly.

My impromptu feet dipping was interrupted by Raul insisting we return to camp and join the others. I couldn't help my cheeriness upon our return, so wanting to relate the waterfall to the others, but during our absence something had obviously occurred as the scene played out before me attested to.

Daniel and Christian were hunched over the laptop, which was cased in something that looked remarkably like something Steve kept his drill in. Whilst David was talking on the satellite phone.

I sat down on one of the camping chairs and Raul took the one next to me. We sat in silence, not wanting to disturb

David, who was talking animatedly to whoever was on the other end of the phone.

Christian acknowledged our return with a quick nod of his head and returned his attention to the screen in front of him. After what seemed like an eternity David cut the call with a curt "Got that over and out."

"Guys, I just need to grab a coffee and I'll bring you all up to speed," David said hurriedly.

Spying the coffee pot on the camping stove I insisted on getting it for him, it smelt good, Haitian coffee was up there with the best I'd ever tasted.

David dived straight in and spoke animatedly, relaying his telephone conversation, as we all sat and listened intently.

"Fuck, we've got a lead already, Robert didn't waste any time after we left and neither did his contact out in the field, basically the guy working undercover with one of the gangs. It looks like a shipment is going ahead tonight. High tide is just after midnight, with a full moon it's perfect conditions for getting the boat out. The bastards have ten kids to transport further up the Caribbean, apparently they're all healthy and the sick fucks expect a good price."

The bile rose in my throat at that last sentence. We had all previously agreed not to let emotions cloud our judgement, it could all so easily lead us into making mistakes that might in turn place us in danger. That we would concede to our emotions once our mission was complete. But it still didn't stop the nausea engulfing me. That human life could be discussed in such a laissez-faire way.

Now was the time for David to put our plan together. He was without doubt the lead player and we deferred to him, especially Christian and I, who had zero experience of covert operations.

Would I be a hindrance? Only now did that thought enter my mind. I'd been so wrapped up with everything going on around me that I genuinely only questioned myself now. Yes, I could use a firearm relatively well, I was fit for my age, I had always kept myself in shape, had a burning rage in my belly to help as many children as we possibly could. Would this be enough to see me through?

For this was without a shred of doubt beyond my comfort zone, beyond anything I'd ever encountered in my whole life, oh for goodness sakes Julia pull yourself together I repeated over and over in my mind, it's too bloody late now for self-recriminations.

Was it divine provenance or just luck that had brought us to this area at this time, I wanted to think it was the former, what were the chances that a shipment was going ahead tonight and not far from where we'd stationed ourselves?

Time was on our side too. It was late afternoon and the area pinpointed by the undercover agent was roughly twenty minutes from camp by car. Raul and Daniel were familiar with the surrounding terrain and this too appeared to be in our favour. Ten minutes out from the beach was an area of forest where we could hide the truck and the approach to the small cove was surrounded with boulders, large enough to conceal us.

The plan was decided, we would head out around 9 pm, giving us plenty of time to recce the area, without fear of the traffickers arriving, get in place and wait.

According to the intelligence dossier, the traffickers were well rehearsed in their shipment strategy. The boat was already waiting in the shallows having been instructed by the gang, who would arrive shortly afterwards by road, the cargo is then marched down the beach and loaded onto the awaiting boat.

So simple, so easy, so incredibly heinous.

It beggared belief it was happening in the twenty first century and not off the coast of Africa three hundred years before, because make no mistake this is modern day slavery wrapped up in a new name, but nonetheless as despicable as what happened to many of these children's' forefathers centuries before. What a cruel twist of fate, that it was now taking place in reverse!

Mankind has learnt absolutely nothing from the annals of history. In fact in my eyes it is so very much worse now, as aren't we supposed to learn from our past crimes and misdemeanours. To make our world a better place, as we are in receipt of the full knowledge of how far man can inflict pain and torture on our fellow world citizens and in particular those who are the most vulnerable, CHILDREN, who cannot defend themselves. No, we have learnt nothing, nothing at all. The devil indeed walks among us, unchecked, free to inflict the most insidious pain on the most innocent.

Chapter 17

Ephesians 5:11 Have nothing to do with the fruitless deeds of darkness, but rather expose them.

The sky was ink black in its intensity, but adorned by millions of stars, and the full moon only added to this magnificent tableau as we made our way to the beach in total silence. The only sound the lapping of the waves rolling onto the sandy shoreline.

David picked up his pace, practically running from where the road led to the sand. Once he'd stopped and began casting his flashlight up and down, highlighting tyre tracks, his need for haste became all too sickeningly apparent. A vehicle had been here and very recently, these were fresh tracks.

He carried on down the beach, with us following, adding our own flashlights, joining his in exposing footprints starting from where the tyre tracks had stopped.

We were too fucking late, what had gone so horrendously wrong? My flashlight had exposed a child's sandal, the type my daughter Lucy loved to wear when she was small. Jelly shoes they'd been called back then. I dropped to my knees in utter desolation, picking it up and cradling it to my chest, subconsciously rocking myself to and fro, as though I were comforting a child. Christian rushed to my side as did the others.

I was completely unable to articulate my words, so just proffered up the sandal for the others to see what I'd found. Something so small and seemingly innocent, had deafeningly signalled our first defeat.

Raul helped me to my feet and dusted the sand off my jeans, such a kind and gentle act amidst the sadness and anger now palpable between us all.

That one little link to the trafficked children had seen our commitment to avoid emotions evaporate instantly.

Apart from David, who had collected himself and was back in stealth mode. "We need to get back to camp ASAP, and find out what the fuck has happened here, there are several scenarios playing out in my head right now, and I don't like any of them."

With that he turned on his heels and marched back up the way we'd come, we all quickly followed like the children of Hamlin after the Pied Piper.

Christian put his arm around me on the walk back, and quietly said, "Come on now, we knew we'd catch a few curve balls, that it wasn't going to be easy and all fall neatly into place, like some movie script. The real world ain't that way."

I replied, "I know, it all sounded too good to be true, but we didn't question it because we put all our faith in whoever it is giving Robert the inside information, but what if this person is playing both sides, you know like a double agent. What happens then, if each lead just takes us on another wild goose chase, or down another rabbit hole?"

"Let's just get back to camp, get our heads together and let David try and ascertain what went wrong, you know there could be a perfectly logical explanation, don't succumb to paranoia just yet." Christian added calmly.

I reluctantly nodded my head in agreement. The trip back was spent in total silence, each of us no doubt trying to answer a plethora of questions inside our own heads before we gave voice to them back at camp.

Me still holding tightly the little sandal, making a silent and defiant vow to the child who had worn it, that we would find her and free her from this hell. To get her and the others to a place of safety and security, as far away from the monstrous creatures who traded innocents like one would buy and sell animals at a livestock market.

An air of stoicism suffused with anger was the only way to best describe our demeanours once we had arrived back at camp.

We clambered out of the SUV, and scrambled in various directions, the headlights illuminating our way. Within minutes the camping lights were on, laptop fired up and David had the satellite phone ready. We worked in total unison, not needing to be told who did what, we were without doubt a team now.

There appeared to be no emails on the laptop, but then it hadn't been that long from discovering the shipment had taken place earlier than we'd been informed to arriving back here. However, David having calibrated the satellite phone was punching in a number, cursing when it didn't connect.

Eventually, after several attempts the phone was answered at the other end. "Robert, can you hear me?"

After what felt like an eternity but in truth was probably only several minutes due to satellite lag Robert answered. David began to relay what had played out at the beach, short and to the point. "They were long gone by the time we got there, just tyre tracks and a kid's shoe left behind, what the hell happened with your lead tonight."

We could gather the gist of the conversation even before David hit the end call dial, and although I could see we were all impatient to ask questions, we waited for David to update us.

"Robert is aware of what happened, but only in so much as an order was given to bring the shipment forward, he only found out afterwards as the undercover agent had no way of contacting him without compromising himself and the whole operation, sometimes split-second decisions have to be made, which we don't necessarily like but which could affect the bigger picture, he'll call again later when he's discovered more information".

I couldn't help myself blurting out "Oh my God, it sounds like what happened during World War Two, we sacrificed Coventry to the Luftwaffe and its bombing blitz, to protect our cracking of the enigma code, too much success would have alerted the Nazis". I felt my cheeks redden instantly at my outburst, but added "You know what my analogy meant, you have to lose some battles to win the war, but that didn't help the casualties of Coventry or the ten children trafficked to God knows where or for what tonight".

David replied, "I get what you're saying and to a certain extent you are correct, however imagine if our mole had been discovered behind some bush or rock communicating the change in plans, the result would have been a bullet to the back of his head, they would know they've been infiltrated, switch operations elsewhere and we wouldn't have a hope in hell of finding them, and hundreds possibly thousands of other kids".

David had treated me gently with his reply and for that I was grateful. Planting myself firmly back in my box I decided to listen rather than participate in the ensuing discussion, whilst reminding myself to engage my brain before I opened my mouth in future. I must compartmentalise my sentiments, something I'd up to now never had a problem doing. In my years as a journalist I've covered many distressing situations, yet been able to go home, cook dinner, read my children their bedtime stories, with them oblivious to the torment I'd witnessed, but this whole situation was beginning to seep into my bones and psyche like an invisible virus, reaching and absorbing every part of my being.

Whilst mulling our next move over copious amounts of coffee and willing the phone to signal an incoming call, Christian was keeping a close eye on the laptop. He raised his arm in an effort to attract our attention, we were instantly silent and gave him our unanimous and undivided attention.

"An email from William Monroe has just come in, I'll read it out,"

"Sources are informing us that there's a significant increase in the amount of cargo coming up from South America, along with locals too. Ergo shipments will be increasing accordingly, the border into the DR is getting too hot so coastal routes being used and some activity detected on Gonave Island, although this is looking more like a holding area. This could go some way to explain the change in tonight's boat leaving earlier than planned, they were in most probability doing another run along the coast. Robert will contact you later with further updated intel, take care. Yours, William".

Daniel was the first to speak. "This has put my mind at rest somewhat, I was greatly concerned that we were deliberately being fed incorrect information, I'm sorry now to have thought this way, but past experiences have left me trusting very few people, present company excluded of course. William Monroe is a good man, God bless him."

We raised our coffee mugs in salute to Daniel's words and I interjected,"I'd like to include Robert too and the undercover agent and whoever else is working behind the scenes to help us." The mugs were raised again in unison and an atmosphere of united solidarity was tangible, enveloping us all in a cloak of comradeship amidst a sea of uncertainty and danger.

The night was beginning to feel endless, as we sat under the black velvet canvas of the sky, I tilted my head to feast on the millions of stars, so many they were almost holding the moon to ransom, fighting for room in the Galaxy millions of miles from here and yet they appeared so close, like some magnificent metropolis, so near and yet so far.

My celestial reverie was interrupted by Christian announcing what he thought our next move should be, given that it was approaching 1 a.m. and no further communication had been received from Robert.

"Guys, it's late and I see no need for us all to sit and wait for a phone call. I suggest we take it in turns to wait up and keep guard, whilst the rest of us get some shut eye. We can't make plans until the intel comes in, so it seems pretty pointless in us all being sleep deprived, we are going to need to be alert and have our wits about us."

No one argued with that. Daniel and Christian volunteered for the first watch. I noticed David walk off towards the truck, he returned bearing two of the berettas we'd been issued with at the Embassy, I hadn't noticed him do this the previous night, did he know something we didn't? He casually passed them to Daniel and Christian, who accepted them without comment.

That thought played over in my mind like Ixion's bloody wheel, as I entered the tent Raul was already in his sleeping bag but thankfully awake. I had to ask him about the guns if I was going to get any chance of sleeping.

"Raul, did you wonder why David brought the guns out tonight and not last night?"

"Actually I did but then quickly thought that perhaps he's just being vigilant, we can't be too careful with traffickers active not far from here. Don't read too much into it my friend, sleep easier in the knowledge we can defend ourselves if necessary."

Raul, always the calm voice of reason had soothed my anxiety like a balm on irritated skin. Yes, I concluded he was absolutely correct in his assessment of the situation and I felt immediately at ease and ready for sleep.

The camp lights had been turned off and the subsequent darkness enveloped me like a shroud, the only movement being the shadows cast by the surrounding trees from the moonlight, they looked like great sentinels keeping guard over us, eerie but nonetheless comforting.

I felt around my sleeping bag for my notepad, pen and flashlight, satisfied they were within easy reach should I have a visit from the spirit realm and I needed to write down any message they might give me. I settled down to sleep, only now noticing the night time serenade of crickets and cicadas, like competing instruments in nature's orchestra, each reaching their crescendo in biphonic fashion, only to commence their playing again and again.

There was no need for the notepad et al as tonight it was just faces that swept across my subconscious, the fleeting and silent images I'd been used to receiving, no pleading for help, only faces. I felt this only served to confirm our failed attempt at rescue the night before, my heart felt as if it were made of lead, it laid so heavy in my chest. I drifted off to a deep but troubled sleep, with these images still fighting for acknowledgement in my mind.

I was dreaming of children playing on a beach, they were laughing and running into the water, dipping their toes and then running toward me as the incoming waves chased them back up the beach. It felt like a scene played out by millions of children the world over, innocence and happiness all rolled into one big bundle of joy. But as I turned my arms outstretched to sweep up one of the children I noticed she was holding out a shoe to me, a little pink jelly shoe, like the one I'd found on the beach earlier, the symbolism hit me like a wrecking ball, causing me to wake from my nightmare.

I took in the scene around me, anxious to concentrate my mind on the here and now, to steady my laboured breathing and thumping heartbeat. Streaks of sunlight were penetrating the tent walls all around me and the air felt cool on my fevered body. I noticed Raul's empty sleeping bag, he must have taken the second watch with David. Me too deep in sleep and dreams to have noticed him leaving the tent.

Rubbing my eyes as if to erase the memory of my nightmare from my body, I made an oath to myself not to mention it to the others. I didn't want them to think I was becoming too emotionally overwrought. I would pull myself together, gather my wits about me and find the strength not to succumb to despondency.

Today was a new day and God willing it would be a positive one for the team. I said a silent prayer for guidance and strength, before I left the tent and joined the others.

A loamy fragrance in the air joined the aroma of coffee and fried bacon, as I approached the circle of chairs I'd left only a few hours before. Raul passed me a plate holding crusty bread filled with the crispy fried bacon, my olfactory senses instantly evoking childhood memories of my Mum frying bacon and the delicious smell of it wafting through the house. My stomach gurgled in appreciation as I took the proffered plate.

"Good morning and thank you Raul, this hotel takes a lot of beating you know," smiling profusely before taking a bite of the much welcome sandwich. My spirits lifting like a phoenix from the ashes.

Before Raul could answer David interrupted; "I need to bring you up to speed with what information we have received overnight. If you don't mind, I'll talk while you eat your breakfast" I nodded my head in tacit agreement.

"The situation is fluid as we knew it would be, and while you were sleeping Robert and William have supplied us with some good intel, and viable ideas/strategies on our next approach."

Chewing and swallowing as quickly as I could without choking myself, I managed an almost strangled reply in my eagerness to express my wish for him to continue immediately.

"Please just tell me everything." Christian and Daniel by this time had joined us. With towels around their shoulders and glistening wet hair I concluded they'd been to the natural pool to bathe. I gave a little wave and smile to acknowledge their return, not wanting to interrupt David by voicing my greetings. They took their seats in silence, giving full attention to David.

"With regards to the outcome from last night, the worry is that we're going to end up chasing our asses at the mercy of those bastards changing times and locations, with our guy unable to make contact and update."

Gathering from the silence of my fellow teammates, I assumed they were already aware of this new information. I'd obviously slept a lot longer than the guys. David continued.

"So, I'm certain you'll agree Julia, we've agreed to heed the advice given and we try and locate the holding areas, reasons being 1. We could possibly discover far more children and 2. the obvious being we negate the possibility of last-minute alterations to their schedules."

"Absolutely yes to all of that, so what's the plan?"

Little over an hour later and with our next move planned and agreed, I made my way to the waterfall. Christian acting as my very own bodyguard, had insisted on accompanying me, totally blowing away my protestations that I'd be totally safe by myself. I'd rather relished the idea of some time on my own, but had conceded defeat when David, Daniel and Raul had added a chorus of disapproval.

In our absence, the others would pack up the camp, load the vehicles and be ready for the off upon our return.

Hastily discarding my clothing I wasted no time and jumped into the pool of water. Christian ever the gentleman had agreed to sit with his back to me, saving my modesty, as although old friends I wasn't about to go naked in front of him.

The shock of the ice-cold water instantly hit every nerve in my body, like a thousand lightning bolts ricocheting around the very depths of me, revitalising me to my core and washing away any vestiges of apathy and self doubt. I felt rejuvenated, a new and strong sense of purpose flowed through my veins on the back of the adrenaline released throughout my body. In short, it felt incredible.

Wanting to stay and indulge longer in this oasis of calm wasn't an option I could luxuriate in. Time was of the essence leading me to hurriedly finish my ablutions and reach for the towel I'd left on the bank of the pool. As I was drying myself and dressing, I couldn't help but share with Christian the positive effect of my ice-cold bath.

"You know, that was just what the doctor ordered, I feel as if I could conquer the world right now, more alive than I've felt in a long while, an epiphany of mind and body is how I'd describe it."

Laughing Christian replied, "Well that's very flowery my dear, but right now get your butt into gear, we've got some exploring to do."

Chapter 18

We were heading for the area between Vertieres and Fort Picolet. With an abundance of archaeological and historical sites, it would yet again provide a near perfect cover for us. From forts to old plantations, the revival of interest in Haiti's rich history was bringing a much needed rise in tourism. Good the more the better as this would enable us to blend in without arousing unwanted attention.

The scenery was breathtaking, from the tree covered mountains to bleached white perfect sandy beaches edging the exquisite turquoise waters of the Caribbean. Rivalling if not surpassing in its beauty, the other Caribbean islands I was more familiar with.

But within all this natural beauty lay a terrifying and hideous evil made manifest by a ruthless and malevolent underbelly of people who sought profit and riches through the pain and suffering of innocents. It was so hard to equate the beauty of this island, so rich in natures finest attributes with the sorrow and fear of children abducted, many from loving families, being held against their will and facing a terrifying future.

Nestled between the mountains and rugged coastline we entered a small township, the approach lined with multi-coloured clapperboard houses although somewhat rundown they were still so synonymous to the Caribbean.

Parked in front of what I took to be the townships only official looking hotel were parked several large, very new and expensive looking vehicles, this immediately drew my attention as they seemed so terribly out of place in this somewhat impoverished looking backwater.

I wasn't the only one who had noticed, the radio instantly sprang to life with David's voice. "Guys, are you clocking the expensive looking automobiles parked out front of that hotel, over?"

Picking up the receiver Daniel answered, "Yes, I copy that David, over and out."

From the back seat I added that I'd made the same observation, that they stood out like a sore thumb, Christian was furiously nodding his head in agreement too.

"Raul and I will park further up and if they leave maybe tail them, over."

Daniel replied, "If you do follow them, may I suggest meeting back up here, as remember we have only the one satellite phone and therefore cannot contact each other, over."

"Yeh, copy that, over and out." With that David was gone and Daniel had parked, before exiting the SUV he reminded us that my name was Linda and checked we had our ID's with us. We had to be careful at all times, especially as there were many corrupt officials in Haiti who could be collaborating with the traffickers.

As we entered what appeared to be the main bar of the establishment the pungent smell of meat cooking assailed our nostrils along with the striking aroma of rhum, it was almost overpowering in its strength.

Daniel indicated an empty table for Christian and I to sit at whilst he headed for the bar.

Trying not to appear obvious I scanned the room but continued my conversation with Christian, desperately trying to keep a relaxed facade when in one corner I noticed and quickly counted six men seated at a round table. Carrying on my casual sweep I surreptitiously kicked Christian's foot under the table.

Six men, hadn't Robert mentioned six men? My heart rate accelerated a little, but determined not to show any interest in them whatsoever carried on my conversation with Christian. He'd obviously noticed them too when we had first entered the room as he gently tapped my foot back.

Daniel joined us at the table bearing a tray with what looked like three coca colas in long glasses. Jovially adding in a slightly louder voice, no doubt for our fellow diners benefit. "I thought it best not to partake of the delicious rhum so early as we have much work to do today and that delicious meat you can smell cooking will not be ready for several hours yet unfortunately."

One of the group raised his head and glared at Daniel, I locked his face away in my memory bank, a face I wouldn't forget, along with his greased back hair and ponytail.

I strained to hear but definitely heard him mutter "It's getting too busy in here" and yes without doubt he had a Spanish accent. One of his cohorts replied "relax my friend," with an American accent, what were the chances of there being two of the nationalities Robert had mentioned around the same table?

My heart was now on overdrive but my head was advising caution and just stay calm and act normal, NORMAL! Who was I trying to kid, nothing about my life in the last few days was remotely normal.

I was brought back to the here and now by familiar voices entering the room, it was David closely followed by Raul. I tempered my surprise by warmly greeting them as they approached our table.

Daniel motioned to the barman for two more drinks and then turned his attention to our friends. "Gentlemen, you're a little earlier than expected." He had his back to the other table so was able to raise an eyebrow without them seeing.

"Yes, fortunately we have found a good trail quicker than we expected, it's all looking good" David informed us as he took a seat.

Well that was pretty cryptic and although I racked my brains I couldn't come up with an answer, patience Julia, patience.

We chatted amongst ourselves and to all intents and purposes gave a portrayal of a group of archaeologists/ historians embarking on some excavation works in the area.

Downing the last of his coca cola David announced that we should be making tracks as he was rather excited to be on our way. Daniel left some notes on the table, waved at the barman and said, "Thankyou e gen yon bon jounen" and we all shuffled out into the midday heat.

Once we were congregated outside David just quickly told us to follow him and Raul to the outside of town. Something was up and I couldn't wait for the short journey to finish and find out what.

Following the truck down a dusty side road we pulled in alongside it and I literally jumped out, my eagerness oozing from every sinew in my body. Christian standing behind me, placed his hands on my shoulders and gave them a light reassuring squeeze, he was as eager as I to hear what David had to say.

"OK Guys, no surveillance needed as I acted on a hunch and placed trackers on two of the vehicles, just wish I'd brought more with me. But seeing those six guys sitting at the table reminded me of the information Robert gave us and I really feel we've struck lucky, you don't get many coincidences like that."

My admiration for David was growing exponentially, he'd thought of every scenario, trackers who'd have thought of that, of course a spook would.

"If and I know it's a big if, they are the traffickers, then those little babies are going to do a lot of the leg work for us, and could possibly lead us to where the children are being held before transit," David added.

After the heartbreak and disappointment of the beach stakeout this news lifted all our spirits, the mood in our little camp was one of cautious optimism and gratitude to David's quick thinking and foresight.

Our next move was a simple one, find a spot to make camp, hunker down and monitor the vehicle movements via the laptop and let them lead us to the holding areas.

I sent a silent prayer for a guiding light, a helping hand, and that may tonight be the night we finally manage to help the children, and just a little plea to keep my incredibly brave and dedicated friends and I safe.

The area was rich in forestation and afforded us a choice of places to settle and wait. After a couple of miles, I saw the truck ahead of us leave the road, we followed down a dusty dirt track strewn with rubble. An abundance of trees lined either side of the track and shortly the narrow expanse opened up to a small clearing, perfect.

David and Raul conveyed to us their idea not to erect the tents, that if it came to it we could always sleep in the vehicles or find a guest house. But ultimately if we were successful tonight a quick getaway might be needed and although they had no qualms about leaving the camping equipment behind, it might be needed later. We all concurred.

All we needed to unload were the camping chairs and some food to see us through the rest of the day and evening and of course the ubiquitous coffee pot.

We spent the ensuing time going over and over again scenarios that might play out in the coming hours. The importance that we were synchronised as a team stressed heavily. David and Daniel would lead the way, with Raul, Christian and I forming the backup behind.

Only David had night vision goggles so it was imperative he lead the way again, but fortunately we would have radio contact between ourselves via headsets, which we tested out and they worked perfectly.

I raised a question "Why didn't we use the headsets at the beach?"

David quickly replied, "The cove was pretty small and the night was clear with the moonlight strong, and we were well covered behind the rocks. Also, Daniel and Raul were familiar with the area, which helped immensely, where we go from now is going to be unchartered territory, we might need to split up over a bigger area, hence the need for radio contact. I hope that answers your question Ma'am."

I opened my mouth to confirm it most certainly did, but before the words were out Daniel exclaimed "They're on the move," he'd been monitoring for tracker movement on the laptop all the while we'd been formulating our plans.

Gathering around him, we stood frozen as we watched the screen in total silence as the trackers did their job and showed us where the vehicles were travelling. David grabbed the land map and spread it out on the camping table, securing it with our coffee mugs as the breeze had picked up.

The feeling passing between us silently was electric, almost tangible the anticipation that this could be our lucky break. Almost childlike I realised I'd subconsciously crossed my fingers, my hands behind my back so to be unnoticeable to the others.

Daniel broke the silence to give David the direction of travel to enable him to follow it on the map. As we watched you could clearly see the two tracker dots, with some distance between them, could the space be the other vehicles without tracking devices, surely this would indicate they were moving as a convoy?

I voiced this question and received a "could well be" from David. After what seemed like an eternity but in reality was probably only twenty minutes or so the vehicles came to a stop.

The guys immediately began to locate the trackers resting place on the far more detailed map. Bingo, they found it and it was as we had thought, one of the old plantation sites.

We quickly discovered that the site had long since been abandoned as an old coffee growing plantation. It contained many stone buildings, among them ironically were ones that were known as the accommodations for the slaves. How history was repeating itself if this place turned out to be where the trafficked children were being held before being dispatched to God knows where.

Remote enough to not attract attention, but within easy reach of the coastal areas known to be hubs used by the traffickers. For all intents and purposes it appeared to be the perfect setting to serve all the requirements needed to run a human slavery route.

Taking the co-ordinates from the map David fired up the satellite phone, informing us he was calling in a few favours as he waited. It turned out the requested favour was for satellite imagery of the plantation. We would be getting a bird's eye view of whatever activity was taking place there, another stroke of genius from our very well-connected spook.

The camp was by now buzzing with a renewed energy, like a battery that had been on a slow charge but was now strengthening to fully loaded. Utterly amazing what a difference just a few hours could make. It was almost tangible, the positivity flowing between us. We had to hold onto to this feeling like ivy wrapped around brickwork, it would give us the strength we would need later.

The satellite imagery we received a short while later was stunning in its revelations. We had indeed found the lair of the snake, laid out before us confirming without doubt that earlier hunches had paid out in spades.

We could clearly see the vehicles that had been parked in front of the hotel in town that morning. The photographs also gave us the layout of the plantation, and comparing them with google images we could see that alterations had been made to several of the dilapidated buildings. Roofs had been added and what looked like steel doors now filled the gaping doorways. There was also an area, heavily fenced, leading off one of the buildings, which shockingly contained what appeared to be children's play equipment, swings and a slide.

It made me feel nauseous, things as innocuous as a child's swing or slide, synonymous with fun, innocence and happiness being used by these heinous bastards to lull the children into a false sense of security, to build trust based on their incessant and nefarious greed.

For a few precious minutes I allowed myself the luxury of recollecting and relishing memories of Lucy, Ethan and Jacob in the garden at home when they were small. The fun, the laughter, the breath caught in my throat as I felt an enormous rush of maternal love course through my veins, mingled with the ever-present guilt at being so far away and in potential danger. I reverted to my mantra, compartmentalise Julia, compartmentalise, it had gotten me through so much in the past, it must and would not fail me now.

Chapter 19

As the night sky darkened and the last vestiges of daylight were chased from the sky we were prepped and ready to go. The plan was to drive and park up as close as possible to the plantation, then make our way on foot to our destination. Thinking ten steps ahead at all times, we were sharply aware that should we be fortunate enough to rescue the children and not knowing what shape they would be in, as short a distance as possible to the vehicles was not only a prerequisite but essential.

We knew from the trackers that two of the vehicles had departed from the plantation, leaving one behind, leading us to surmise that, why would a vehicle be left?, this must indicate the imminent arrival of a shipment or so we all hoped and prayed.

We were all perfectly aware that we were winging it, but lady luck must at one point cast her affections our way, especially if the power of prayer played any part in it.

Each one of us were praying as if our lives depended on it even David, which in truth they did, coupled with the sheer strength of our convictions and a determined spirit to right the wrongs meted out to the countless children preyed upon by monsters.

David tapped his watch, the signal for Go Go, we duly made our way to the vehicles, falling in step one behind the other. When we reached them David handed out the berettas, I've never felt more grateful to be in the possession of a gun, I duly stashed it in the back of my jeans, emulating the guys. Our little troupe of soldiers, going off once more into the unknown.

"One more thing," David added, "I want you all to wear one of these, a balaclava, I need to cover every scenario and if things go wrong and they see us and get away, there would be one helluva bounty on your heads, especially Daniel and Raul."

Even after that sobering statement of David's it was quite amazing how energetic I felt given I'd had such little rest, it must be pure adrenaline coursing through my veins. I guessed it must be the same for the guys too.

Christian and I would travel with David, leaving Raul and Daniel bringing up the rear and as the night crept in on silent feet, and with just a frisson of apprehension in the air, we were off into the night.

Although small in physical numbers, we were strong and determined, united at heart with a ring of invisible steel wrapped around us, like an umbilical cord connecting babies in the womb, an unbreakable bond.

The air was humid and a cacophony of cicadas greeted us as we exited the vehicles. We were approximately fifteen minutes on foot from the perimeter of the plantation, as near as we dared to chance, however still closer than originally planned, the weather was on our side, the terrain dry and accessible.

With a last brief run through of "the plan" and equipment check, we began to make our way to the plantation.

Fortunately, it was a clear and starry night, this and the moonlight lent a helping hand, making our trek that much easier and safer. In total silence we followed David, only stopping when his raised arm indicated the perimeter fencing.

From the satellite images we'd scanned earlier, this fencing was another positive indicator of abnormal activity in the area. These plantations had been abandoned for decades, with anything of value looted, ergo, why would what appeared to be new fencing be needed?

Removing a small pair of wire cutters from his backpack, David made light work of cutting an access/exit route through the metal, wide enough to enable several people to escape simultaneously. Once inside the plantation grounds and with bushes for cover we retrieved our covert two-way earpieces from our backpacks and David donned the night vision goggles, only after making a note of our co-ordinates.

My earpiece came to life with David's voice, requesting acknowledgement that we could hear him, with a thumbs up from the rest of the team and a "keep it tight" instruction from David we began our mission.

Through many years of neglect the ground was abundant in undergrowth and trees, resulting in our cautious but steady pace, however it wasn't long before David broke the silence.

"OK guys, I'm making out the start of the outbuildings, stay here and I'll recce ahead, over and out."

Huddling behind some bushes it seemed like an eternity before David returned and we eagerly awaited his findings.

"Something is definitely going down, there are lights on in several buildings and lots of voices, I'd say at least six hostiles, and from their chatter they're not here to discuss coffee. There are a few disused buildings, just shells, but they will give us enough cover and a place to wait. The aerial footage was a Godsend, you've seen the layout now memorise it and put the balaclavas on, follow me and hunch down."

We followed David's instructions and hunched down, silently making our way to one of the outbuildings, it was literally just four walls, no roof or door and grass underfoot, but good cover nonetheless.

Breathing deeply to try and steady my nerves, my heart beating like a huge timpani drum, it felt as if it would at any moment burst forth from my chest. My hands were shaking and clammy too, get a bloody grip woman I told myself, don't get this far and dissolve into a quivering heap. It did the trick, my momentary wobble coming under control, I made yet another silent gesture of thanks to the "big man upstairs." He was on our side tonight, I just instinctively knew it.

Part of the plan was David's insistence that we not use our names to communicate with each other. Instead we would have call signs, to make it easier for the less initiated, they were to be very simple, literally just numbers. David would be "one", Daniel "two", Raul "three", Christian "four" and myself "five".

Hearing David's hushed voice through my earpiece asking, "You OK number five?" brought me back to the here and now, whispering, "All good here." I swear that man had telepathic abilities, that or an incredible sense of smell, like he could sniff the adrenaline that had momentarily coursed through my veins.

After what seemed to me like an eternity of time, of surreal blackness, a void of any contact, sound or movement, the maelstrom commenced. Reflecting afterwards I can only describe my reflexes as being on autopilot, yes that's the only way I can accurately depict it and comprehend it in my own mind.

Chapter 20

Psalm 82:3-4
Give justice to the weak and the fatherless; maintain the right of the afflicted and the destitute. Rescue the weak and the needy; deliver them from the hand of the wicked.

It started with the arrival of what we surmised were several vehicles, their engines clear and loud in the quietness of the night, the diesel fumes pervading the scent of the wild oleander and other flora. From the general noise, a larger, heavier vehicle could be heard. That and raised voices, much shouting, thinking themselves far from anywhere and safe, believing they were unheard by anyone but each other.

We all simultaneously and in unison whispered to each other our thoughts that this could be carrying cargo. Oh how I loathed that term, but be that as it may, it was how the movement of children was labelled.

Through my earpiece David's voice came, the beacon that we had all been waiting for "This is it guys, hang a right out of here, keep low and in formation, watch each other's backs and it's a go to rescue these kids."

One by one we filed out of the little derelict building which had been our hiding place, each clutching a piece of clothing from the one in front of us, as an umbilical cord connecting each to the other.

With David leading, we made it to the next outbuilding, standing for a few welcome seconds to rest our backs. Then onto the next, repeating this until we reached the entrance to the main atrium of the old plantation. Where once would have stood huge gates, it was just a gaping access.

Once again my earpiece sprang to life with David's voice, whispering that he was going to cross the accessway to the other side, the shadows of the walls giving him good cover, crouching he sprang the short distance and requested that number "two" cross on his signal of "go".

Upon hearing number "two" Daniel crouching, made his way to join David. With Raul ahead of Christian and I, we had lookouts on both sides of the entrance. Still in shadow, affording us good cover we waited and listened intently, as I sent up a silent prayer that no more vehicles would arrive and discover us surveilling them.

My prayer was answered, as after what seemed only a few minutes the engines were turned off, but the headlights kept on, these and the lighting from the buildings meant we were able to discern the voices more clearly and audibly, yet from the light David and Daniel were able to watch and monitor the situation without having to get closer and unnecessarily endangering our cover.

It appeared Lady Luck was on our side once again, as English was being spoken albeit broken. I hastily presumed that as we were already aware from the cafe, these traffickers hailed from French speaking Haiti and Spanish speaking South America and English would in all likelihood be common to both. Yet another silent prayer of thanks was sent skywards, as my French was good but my understanding of the Spanish language was dismal.

We had covered so many scenarios in our pre-planning, but the main one being that should all go to plan and we found ourselves in this situation, we would wait for the 'cargo' to be unloaded and safely taken to a holding area before we took action, to avoid at all cost injury to any of the children. Utmost in our minds was the total safety of these victims of utter cruelty and evil.

As if on cue, we all clearly heard the shouted words of "get them out now". Clearly heard was the sound of steel doors being opened, the grind of steel on steel and then the shudder of metal as the doors were set free.

Then the voices, voices that until the day I die I will never forget, forever etched in my memory, like indelible ink, there forever to remind me that good can conquer evil, when you have enough faith to carry through on your convictions, even when you are frightened and unsure, you must listen to your inner self and believe you can make a difference in the face of much adversity. Never be afraid to question and fight for what you think is righteous. David and Goliath is a sound analogy, to attest to this.

Back to the unfurling situation as I recall it. I say voices, but in reality it was crying, the frightened cries of terrified children being herded like cattle from the back of a truck by the vile creatures who saw them only as a commodity, to be sold like meat in a market, by jackals, preying like vultures on the vulnerable and unprotected children, sending them to uncertain futures, be it into the sex trafficking trade, organ harvesting or God knows what else the depraved of this world require to fulfil their pitiful existence.

Quietly David conveyed to us that he had counted twelve children had been moved from the truck to the holding area, a number we could easily transfer in our vehicles and on the count of five for him to begin the assault. That there were eight hostiles, he and Daniel had eyes on six, the other two still being involved in herding the cargo to the holding pen. No firearms were in view, they were obviously comfortable that this would be a straightforward transfer, but to be in no doubt they were armed.

What transpired from then on would not have seemed out of place from a Hollywood action movie, only this would involve real ammunition and real death.

The countdown arrived and to coin a phrase, 'all hell broke loose'. I could see David spring forward and drop to the ground, closely followed by Daniel, with Raul motioning for us to stay put. I heard the first round of gunfire quickly followed by a scream of what I took to be agony, then a second followed rapidly by a third and fourth, equally accompanied by screams. With a motion from Raul for Christian and I to follow him we entered the fray, emulating David and Daniel we dropped to the ground, on our stomachs ready to assess the situation and take aim.

The act of surprise had worked out brilliantly, I could easily make out two hostiles on the ground and apparently unmoving, the smell of gunpowder all invading our senses of smell, acrid in its intensity. Fortunately little smoke was emitted, giving us a clear view of what was unfolding before us.

Another hostile emerged from one side of the truck, only to be felled before he could raise his gun, three down, five to go! Adrenaline was kicking in now, that fight or flight instinct, the former being the only course of action I was intent on, along with my "band of brothers in arms."

I could see David & Daniel were up and running, keeping low, both hands clasped around their firearms and weaving to try and escape returning fire from the hostiles.

David and Daniel being ahead were giving much needed cover, they were far more adept and obviously far better trained in armed combat than us.

But as I rose to my feet behind Raul and Christian all my attention was focused on what was in front of me, fatal mistake, that and I hadn't retrieved my gun from the waistband of my jeans. From my right side lunged a hostile brandishing a large knife, in a split second and seemingly out of nowhere the Krav Maga training flooded my brain.

Oh Lucy how would I ever repay you, her insistence that I join the classes I'd booked to keep my adored daughter safe, were now going to save me. Immediately correcting my posture, instinct and the primal need to survive took over. Taking the basic outlet stance and using the balls of my feet to anchor myself as firmly as possible given the uneven terrain, elbows in and hands out. Within seconds my assailant swung the knife, arms together and with all my strength I struck sideways, he dropped the knife and I followed through with an almighty knee to his groin.

As he fell to the ground, I quickly retrieved his weapon and for good measure I kicked him hard in the throat, as he lay writhing in agony. I drew my gun but try as I might I couldn't shoot the bastard, some innate sense of my right to take a human life was clouding my judgement.

The decision deftly and decisively taken out of my hands as Raul reached my side and discharged two bullets to the head.

Silent, Raul grabbed my arm and urged me forward, thankfully with no admonishment for my inability to pull the trigger, not that one would be needed should the situation arise again. As flashbacks to the children's' cries brought me to my senses, plus the stone cold reality that the now dead hostile would not have hesitated in dispatching me. A truly sobering thought if any were needed.

Calculating that the body count was now four down with four to go and keeping that in mind I re-joined the ensuing battle.

Christian managed a brief nod and a thumbs up sign as I reached his side. There wasn't time for any further communication as David's voice came through our earpieces.

"One and two are still good, three, four, five confirm all OK?" We duly gave the affirmative.

With that more gunfire could be heard, but I was unable to make out if it came from us or them. Hearing "take that you bastard" I thought could safely take the tally to five, with three to go.

We were now approaching the main building, when an engine from one of the vehicles could be heard revving up, Raul reacted immediately, sprinting to the vehicle in question, Christian and I spread out and followed to give him cover, safe in the knowledge that David and Daniel were dealing with the remaining two hostiles.

It was all happening at lightning speed and like nothing I had ever experienced in my life before and hopefully never would again, but alarmingly at the same time I was feeling exhilarated too, a myriad of emotions experienced in such a short time.

Raul had reached the vehicle in question, ferociously grabbing the driver's door and completely startling the hostile inside, he dived in and began trying to haul him out. Christian reading the situation superbly, made for the left-hand passenger door, ripping it open and executing a punch to the hostile's head, swiftly followed through by a second blow.

Raul dragged the now quite limp hostile from the vehicle to the ground, he fell onto his stomach and climbing onto his back, quickly exclaimed "we want this bastard alive" peering over at the semi-conscious man on the floor I could see it was none other than "ponytail". The one we had concluded was the head honcho of this sick band of human traffickers.

Retrieving cable ties from a pocket of his cargo pants, he pulled his quarry's arms onto his back and deftly tied them together, good and tight. For good measure he removed a scarf like bandana from around Ponytail's neck and used it as a makeshift gag.

Rejoining us, Christian held up a gun that he had retrieved from the vehicle, thank God and all that's holy the hostile hadn't had the time to use it. We would keep this weapon for later, as it might yield important information as to who was providing the weaponry for the traffickers.

David once again coming through our earpieces, "Two hostiles who entered the building are dead, number two and I are now exiting the building, over."

Before any of us could reply David and Daniel appeared at our sides. "Well that makes seven in my reckoning," David added as he assessed Ponytail, still semi-conscious on the ground.

Raul hastily informed him of the hostile we'd taken out, so the tally was in fact eight.

Removing our balaclavas, which was an enormous relief, we afforded ourselves some quick high fives, before David turned off his earpiece and we could actually now talk to each other properly.

"That went better than I had hoped, quick, clean and we're all in one piece," gesturing towards our captive he asked, "Who took that dude down?"

Raul responded, "It was a team effort, pure and simple."

David adding, "Now onto the rescue phase, pdq, we don't know if any of these bastards managed to communicate with outsiders."

We knew we must move rapidly now, the children were already traumatised and hearing the gunfire would only terrify them further. Raul was instructed with Daniel's help to tie Ponytail's ankles together, we didn't want this bastard escaping once he regained full consciousness. His capture would hopefully reap rewards of information later.

Frankly I didn't give a damn how information would be extracted from him, how much inflicted pain it would take to make this canary sing. I was in no doubt as to David's probable repertoire of how to make him talk and I was completely cool with it, in fact I would request a front row seat when it took place.

With Raul and Christian staying behind to guard our quarry, the rest of us headed to the 'holding pen'. We had all agreed unanimously prior to the start of the mission and during the pre-planning that a woman's presence would, should we be fortunate enough to actually rescue some children, surely be a comfort to frightened innocents.

Also covered was the possibility of taking one of the hostiles captive, and although in my heart of hearts I felt that would prove impossible, we had achieved it, and we had taken the numero uno of this outfit. Albeit I was not naive enough to think we had the head of the snake, he was an integral part of the trafficking cartel, of that I also had no doubt in my mind.

Mixed emotions traversed my brain as we made our way, one was eagerness to reach the children, but intertwined with this was trepidation at what sights we were about to encounter, and doubts that I would have the cognitive ability to be a positive force and not succumb to sadness and anger. I was only human after all.

With the help of flashlights illuminating our way, yet casting eerie shadows on our path, we reached the holding pen in just a few minutes. No sounds emanated from it, just deafening silence.

Daniel spoke in French not Haitian Creole "n'ayez pas peur, nous sommes la pour vous emmener en securitie" (do not be afraid we are here to take you to safety), then added "Mon nom est Raul et je vais deverrouiller la porte, veuillez prendre du recul." (My name is Raul, and I am going to unlock the door, please stand back.").

Easing the large bolt open slowly and carefully so as not to add further fear to the little ones, Raul then gently opened the door and shone his flashlight into the pen. David stood to the other side of the door and added his flashlight to give us a better view of the interior.

With a deep breath I made my way inside. The scene that filled my senses was pitiful, they were all huddled in one corner and only now did the whimpering begin, slowly at first then rising in its intensity.

I don't know what kicked in first, my natural empathy as a Mother, that overpowering need to protect the defenceless or my sense of righting this horrendous wrongdoing, but whatever it was I took control of the immediate situation facing me.

In a quiet, soothing and even tone I began.

"Mon non est Julia, et avec ces bon hommes je suis la pour vous aider, nous devons nous depecher pour vous mettre en securitie, s'il vous plait les petits nous font confiance et suivez nous maintenant." (my name is Julia, and I along with these good men are here to help you, we must hurry to get you to safety, please little ones trust us and follow us now).

I automatically opened my arms and just two initially came forward, this opened the floodgate and the remainder followed, all trying to get into my arms. I almost toppled over with the stampede, shocked at how easily their trust had been placed in me, how desperate they were for salvation.

Regaining my balance I uttered just a few calming words and managed to touch each ones' hands as they reached out to me. My heart was literally bursting, but my head urged the utmost speed.

Gently, all the while reassuring them, I gave instructions on how to exit the pen. To form a line, one in front of the other, and to take hold of the one immediately in front of them, showing how to do it as I spoke.

With David leading and Daniel at the rear we were off, me with the youngest holding so tightly to my hand, desperate not to let go. Estimating she was no older than six, I bent and scooped her up in my arms, wrapping her little legs around my hips and burying her head in my neck, we were ready.

Slowly but surely, we made our way to the others. I quietly uttered words of encouragement along the way, a continuous repetition of comforting words. I was truly amazed at how easily they had put their trust in us, relieved but saddened at the same time.

Before we reached Christian and Raul, David paused and told the children to wait. "I don't want the kids seeing that shitbag we captured, wait here I won't be long."

It was Raul who returned to our sides, informing us that David would be taking the captive back in his very own vehicle and that we should rendezvous where we had hidden ours.

Cautiously making our own way back, we reached the hole in the fencing which had been cut out earlier and we all duly filed through it.

The children were silent, just meekly following one another, but I continued to offer comforting words, not stopping, until we reached the vehicles.

Chapter 21

We had managed the first dangerous leg of our mission with thankfully no injuries sustained to us or the children. Taking just a brief moment I sent up yet another silent prayer of thanks and gratitude to the big Guy in the sky.

Christian was already there, with the captive nowhere in sight nor his vehicle. He quickly explained that they had him securely restrained in the cab of his own truck and David was currently driving him back to base camp. He wouldn't be seen by the children, and that there was plenty of room to now load the children.

It was hastily worked out that eight would go into the cargo bed of the truck, with Raul overseeing them, and Christian driving. That left Daniel to drive the SUV, I would travel in the back, with the little one I had carried on my lap and the remaining three by my side.

We had to get the children away as quickly as humanly possible, the alarm would soon be raised and no doubt back - up dispatched. Once the realisation had set in that we had not only taken their precious cargo but had killed their fellow traffickers, we would be hunted down without mercy.

We were under no illusions whatsoever, that if we were to be successful, it might possibly come at a huge price to our personal safety. With the luxury of hindsight perhaps I hadn't thought that part through enough in the beginning, given it much credence, acknowledged just who we would be going up against, perhaps I had been naive?

However here we were putting the second leg of our plan into motion as we headed off. It would be light all too soon and it was imperative we get the children to a place of safety immediately.

I'd bandied the genesis of an idea to the guys several days earlier, and to my surprise they all thought it was a sound one. Not wanting to travel too far by road for fear of running into hostiles coming to the aid of their partners in crime was a very real possibility. Until help arrived, we would have to take the children to a nearer place of safety.

Maybe I'd watched too many movies, but at the time it just made good sense to me.

When we had made one of our camps and I'd swam in the pool by the waterfall, I'd noticed and commented on the cave that appeared to be behind the cascading water. We investigated it and sure enough there was indeed quite a large cavern, hidden from immediate view.

Yes, the access was slippery almost precarious, but by forming a human chain from the bank of the pool, with two of us standing on the almost submerged boulders that were situated to the side of the cave's entrance, then with one of us stationed just inside, we might pull it off. Correction we would bloody well pull it off.

It was damp for several feet inside, but much drier the farther you ventured into the interior. At least it was safe, affording us a few vital hours to contact William back at the Embassy and for reinforcements to arrive.

David had saved the location into the GPS, enabling a straightforward run to our destination. During the journey I was conscious of how deathly quiet the children were, not at all surprising given the ordeal they had all been enduring, not only the frantic rescue, but days maybe weeks prior to it. God only knew what they had witnessed and been subjected too. With that in mind I continued with a constant stream of soft reassurances and occasionally I would reach across and give a physical touch to each in turn. The little girl on my lap still clung to me like a vine, I gently stroked her hair, and rocked her as best I could, as I had many times with my own children, whether it be after they'd grazed a knee or awoken from a bad dream, the universal act of empathy from a mother figure must surely work its magic, oh how I was praying it would.

As the SUV came to a final stop and the ignition turned off, Daniel got out of his seat and came around to the other door, I gently instructed the three children to leave the vehicle and to wait with Daniel whilst I manoeuvred my own exit with the little girl still wrapped around me.

The children from the truck were already waiting, guarded over by Christian and Raul. David was still in the cab with our hostage, what was the plan for him? I couldn't recall, my mind so completely taken up with concern for the children, I didn't waste another thought, confident in the knowledge that David would have it covered.

Now that there was less need for urgency I asked if anyone needed to pee, several hands were raised immediately, asking for a flashlight I led them to a nearby tree and instructed them to relieve themselves and that I was going to stay and not leave them.

Once we were all congregated together, I could take a more intense scrutiny of the children gathered before us. They varied in height and, as with most children ascertaining ages can be difficult. I would leave questioning them until later, once we had them secure and further trust gained, for now we had to put the next step into operation and that was getting them into the cave and giving them food and drink. Whatever we had would have to be shared, but the priority must be the children.

Handing over to Daniel and Raul, whose French was obviously far better, they began to explain what was going to happen next. I was incredibly touched with how tenderly both men handled the situation, the children kneeling on the ground before them were still silent but did manage to acknowledge by nodding when asked if they understood what we were asking of them.

The truck would be driven as close to the pool as possible, to save time having to ferry our supplies, sleeping bags and camping gear etc. But where was our captive going to be kept? Posing this question to David, he took me to one side and briefly explained that he had been transferred to the SUV, and given a "little something" to help him sleep. Roughly translated, he'd been drugged to keep him nice and quiet until our backup arrived. Sounded good to me, keep him comatose until the guys needed to extract vital information from the son of a bitch. Then hand him over to the relevant authorities or maybe he would be transferred to some black ops site, either option was ok with me.

Daniel was to stay behind with the SUV, David instructed him to put his earpiece back in, that once the children were safely in the cave, he was to bring the SUV to the pond.

Luckily, we had the camping lamps, they helped light our way, along with the headlamps from the truck ahead of us, it didn't feel as scary as it would have in total darkness.

Now came the trickiest part, positioning the camping lamps and directing the truck's headlamps to illuminate the waterfall, we began to get in place to transfer the children to the cave.

Raul volunteered to be the first to venture forth, he would station himself at the side of the waterfall on the edge, ready to take a child passed to him by Christian, passed to him in turn by David, I would be on the pond's bank, passing to David.

Tenderly encouraging the little one in my arms to let go of me and to stand by my side, we all watched with bated breath for Raul to safely make his way. At one point there were gasps from us as Raul slipped and almost landed in the water. Regaining his balance admirably, he made it, turning to give the thumbs up sign, it was now Christian's turn, successfully reaching his post in the chain, he gave the thumbs up sign too. Now over to David, he didn't have far to go. Bingo, we were ready to start passing the children down the line.

Gingerly the first child stepped forward, taking her in my arms I carefully made my way to the banks edge and leaning slightly I passed her to David's awaiting arms. With my heart in my mouth I watched as he tentatively sidled along to pass her onto Christian, who easily passed his precious package to Raul.

Releasing the breath I'd held in, I glanced around at the waiting children and gave them my best smile, hoping to give courage and reassurance. The next child came forward for me to begin the process again, this one was older and slightly heavier, I struggled momentarily, gaining my balance, but the little one in my arms had felt my slight wobble and clung tighter to me, seeing this David edged slightly nearer to me and opened his arms wide, the encouragement worked and I passed her into his awaiting arms.

On and on this went until eleven of the children were safely transferred to the cave. This left just the little bird who had not left my side. Bending to take her in my arms, I couldn't help it, I planted a kiss on the top of her head and gently squeezed her before whispering "allez peu her son votre etre une fille courageuse maintenant." (come on little one it's your turn to be brave now).

Holding her tightly, I moved forward, with no hesitation at all she let me transfer her to David's arms. She maintained eye contact with me, her sad but beautiful little eyes not leaving mine until she was safely with Raul.

David and Christian made their way back to where I was standing, now it was my turn to make my way across the slippery boulders, praying that I wouldn't fall into the water I took my first step, geez, they were indeed slippery, not wanting to make a fool of myself, I didn't hesitate, instead planting one firmish foot in front of the other I ventured forth. I made it.

Raul had ushered the children towards the back of the cavern. Along with his flashlight, he had a camping lamp which gave us just enough light to make the place appear less daunting and traumatising for the children.

Within twenty minutes give or take, the Guys had brought the camping gear and food stuff to us. Spreading the sleeping bags out as best I could I beckoned the children to sit and asked if any were hungry or thirsty, twelve little arms were raised instantly, reminding me of little birds in a nest, eager for when their parents return with nourishment. I beamed a huge smile in response, my heart surging, that they felt safe enough now to accept the offer of vittles.

Rummaging through the two coolers and boxes, I found bread, bananas and milk. These would do for now, surely all children liked banana sandwiches with warm milk, I know my three used to lap them up.

As I busied myself preparing the food and firing up the camping stove I noticed David, Christian and Raul were deep in conversation. My interest was piqued, seeing me observing them David just nodded his head and mouthed "it's all good." Content, I carried on.

There was only enough for one slice each and half a cup of warm milk (thank goodness we'd bought enough paper cups and plates on our shopping expedition) but at least it was something. The children were showing signs of tiredness now, gesturing sleep with my hands and nodding, they began to settle.

There would be time enough later to prise information from them, to find the answers we all wanted desperately to know. For now, rest was essential. With that I joined the guys, I could smell coffee brewing and boy did I need one, the stronger the better as I was beginning to succumb to weariness myself.

"You are a natural with children Julia," Raul said as I stood by him, "I can now understand why you were chosen to have the gift of sight, to be an Earth Mother as you call it."

My eyes filled with tears and my bottom lip began to tremble as I replied. "Thank you, Raul," that was all I managed to utter, my distress evident. Before I knew it Christian was wrapping his arms around me, an all encompassing embrace. It was just what I needed, and I took much solace from this act of kindness.

"We're almost there sweetheart, come on dry your eyes, drink some coffee and get that bulldog spirit back, you're going to need it for the next stage." How did Christian know exactly the right words to say at the right time, many years of friendship I guess!

Clearing his throat to garner my attention David began to update me on the developing situation. I sensed he was uncomfortable with female emotions and perhaps the supernatural too.

I learned that he had used the satellite phone to contact William and had requested assistance in moving the children to a place of safety.

With corruption so rife in Haiti, that place of safety would initially be the American Embassy. Too much money had passed hands with top officials paid handsomely to turn a blind eye to and often facilitate in the human trafficking trade. It was as we were all too aware a very lucrative business and locating a safe house could prove difficult.

Once safely back at the Embassy, debriefing would commence. For now though, we just had to rely on good old Uncle Sam to come to our rescue and pray to God we weren't discovered by the bad guys in the meantime.

The plan was to lie low until sunrise, less attention would be given to the movement of vehicles in daylight.

By now that was only a couple of hours away and with the united encouragement of the guys I shut my eyes and willed sleep to come, if only for an hour, that would recharge my depleted battery somewhat. The physical and mental turmoil had taken its toll, I felt exhausted, drained.

Chapter 22

As I surfaced from my deep, untroubled but far too brief slumber, I discovered the little one who had clung to me so closely during the rescue, had climbed onto my lap. Still sleeping, with her head on my chest, she was curled up and I had wrapped my arms around her, cocooning her. I acknowledged to myself that I was becoming too attached, but how could you not? My own children had flown the nest and it felt so innately good to be needed again, in the way only little ones wanted and needed a maternal touch.

David was once again issuing instructions. I could see all the camping gear had been cleared away, leaving just the children huddled on the sleeping bags.

Urging the little one in my arms to wake up, I was yet again astounded at the trust she had so easily placed in me as she sidled off my lap and waited by my side for me to rise from the chair. Taking hold of her little hand, giving it a gentle squeeze of reassurance, we readied ourselves to vacate the cave.

Emerging into the outside world to be greeted by a plethora of bird song and warmth on our skin we began to make our way back to the bank of the pond. Once again forming a chain to transfer the children, we began the process.

After stopping for toilet breaks, we made our way to the clearing to be met by a somewhat incongruous sight.

Rather than send the ubiquitous fleet of large black SUV's, synonymous of officialdom, William had arranged for the Haitian equivalent of a Dairy Queen delivery truck for transportation back to the Embassy.

A simply ingenious plan, who would question a food truck? These guys were masters at deception. I was truly in awe of them.

I travelled in the back of the food truck with our precious load, accompanied by Raul who was far more able to converse between French and Haitian Creole than I.

It seemed like an eternity had passed before the doors of the truck were finally opened to reveal the sanctuary of the Embassy. Never in my entire life had I been so grateful for the view my eyes were now drinking in.

As a sentient being, eager to quench my thirst, I gorged on the beautiful sight before me, and on one person in particular, Robert. Making eye contact with me, he doffed his hat and made to bow, no doubt in acknowledgement to the success of our mission.

Eagerly jumping down from the back of the truck, turning round to grab my little one, I made my way to Robert, bypassing all the others standing there with blankets and bottled water.

"My dear girl against all odds you did it," were the only words I heard before I fell into his outstretched arms.

"Yes, we did it Robert, it's only a start, but we did it." I was certain there would be more than enough time later for us to reconnect, for the time being our priority must be the immediate welfare of the children.

I was far too aware we'd only rescued twelve out of possibly thousands, but perhaps now the realisation that it was possible, with grit, determination and an overwhelming sense of justice, that maybe, just maybe we could start to eradicate the evil of human trafficking. Because if a middle-aged woman from the suburbs can set that in motion, anything is possible, and it bloody well could be.

If Gladys Aylward could do it all those years ago in China, with modern technology and the right people in place, we could do it now. My feeling of omnipotence might be fleeting, but it felt damn good.

The ensuing hours were initially filled with the welfare of the children. A room within the Embassy was hastily altered to accommodate them, camp beds were set and even teddy bears were present on each of them. A small token, but what child didn't find a teddy bear comforting?

During all of this uppermost in my mind was the debriefing facing us and the ramifications we might all be facing. After all, we had carried out a mission on foreign soil, a matter not taken lightly by most powers at be, an international storm could well be the outcome we all feared.

After seeing to the needs of the children, we all were given the luxury of a shower, a change of clothes, food and rest. Around midday, leaving several Embassy staff to watch over the children I joined the others in the meeting room we had originally gathered in just a few days before, but which felt in all honesty a lifetime ago. Present were William the Ambassador, our little band of brothers, Robert and several other individuals I wasn't familiar with.

After the introductions I learned that one of the attendees was from the US State department, another a high ranking official from the Haitian government, and in turn officials from the Governments of Guatemala, Bolivia and Colombia, it felt as if I were sitting in front of the United bloody Nations. But determined to hold my own counsel, I listened intently to what they had to say.

They in turn filled a whole void of unanswered questions and more. It turned out that "Ponytail" was none other than a most wanted individual, his real name being Luis Ramirez, a one-time big player in the narcotics trade, having now switched his nefarious activities to human trafficking, a far more lucrative and in demand trade.

What followed made me want to retch, Christian sitting to my left reached for my hand and didn't let go.

Not only were these children destined for the sex trade market, but also for much darker uses. Organ harvesting and to be used in what can only be described as sacrificial offerings to certain sick bastards, who adhered to the dark practises of worship to ungodly deities, the horror of that last statement leaving me stunned and unable to articulate a response.

The guy from the State Department rose to his feet and walked towards a laptop positioned on a table, in front of this was a projector screen, asking for the lights to be dimmed he proceeded to a brief presentation. The contents of which will haunt me for the rest of my days.

Suffice to say "adrenachrome" will be forever etched in my memory, like a vile, sordid tattoo, it may fade a little over time, but would always be there to remind one of an event in their life.

As much as I had researched the "market" for trafficking, and whose sick needs were met by this insidious and heinous trade, this element had evaded me, not now, fully informed I felt sick to my soul. Nectar to the rich and elites of this world, their need for it was satisfied by the abduction of innocent children, children who wouldn't be missed.

The heart breaking reality struck me, as if a giant wrecking ball had taken a direct hit on my body and psyche. An all engulfing anger and sadness filled me with equal measure. To hell with keeping an outward facade of calm, I truly felt that I could rip these monster's limb from limb and not feel one shred of sympathy to the agony I inflicted.

Taking a quick glance around the others in the room, it confirmed to me that they felt exactly the same. The anger was palpable, emanating from us all, like molten lava, gathering momentum as it slithered down the side of an erupting volcano, gaining force as it made its way, clearing all flotsam and jetsam in its path.

Enough of portraying our anger, now onto what our collective response would be. How going forward, we would begin to formulate a plan to get to the head of the snake. To open the floodgates of not only eradicating this enormous scourge on humanity, but with a huge amount of faith we could bring awareness to the public.

The latter would come much later, for now would we go hunting for the perpetrators of pure evil.

Chapter 23

It was imperative that we draw the next phase to conclusion quickly. We'd managed against all odds to spring the element of surprise to a part of the trafficking concerning the movement of cargo. Now with the enemy alerted we had to strategically plan our next moves. As much as humanly possible to dot every I and cross every single T, we were attempting to play 5 D chess with some of the most evil and cunning people on this sacred planet. We must cover every eventual scenario, second guess their moves and outwit them.

With that uppermost in our minds, it was time to pay "Ponytail" a visit. He had been secured in the depths of the Embassy, in a scene reminiscent of an episode of CSI, we were taken to a part of the building that was completely off radar, that didn't exist in the protocols of all things diplomatic.

It hadn't taken long to ascertain "Ponytails" identity. He was confirmed as Luis Ramirez, a born and bred Colombian. An infamous major player in the narcotics trade, who it appeared had been one of the first to realise there was a new sheriff in town, one who was hell bent on closing the lucrative opioid trade that had been given free rein to flood North America with drugs that would see a sizeable amount of the population dependant on the addictive filth he could easily distribute without fear nor retribution.

How easy it would be to flood the porous borders of North America from Texas to California and its coastal regions with "refugees" seeking a better life for kith and kin. Using this as a cover to traffic children needed to satisfy the needs of sick individuals. Better still to use people seeking refuge as parentis in absentia.

These sick and twisted bastards had it all worked out, the perfect cover to move children at will to God knew what fate awaited them.

What they hadn't anticipated was that along with narcotics, human trafficking was and truly on the radar of a new administration.

To prey on parents who would be willing to pay whatever price to ensure their children would be given a place in a country where their safety would be assured. Coupled with this the opportune event of an earth shattering earthquake, that would see the displacement of thousands of vulnerable children, that amid the ensuing chaos would not be missed or accounted for.

With all of this in mind, I was eager to witness the interrogation of our captive. I wasn't disappointed, in fact I allowed myself several minutes of self-indulgent praise, a vanity I know, but one well deserved as he was indeed singing like the proverbial canary.

In exchange for witness protection he was willing to share everything he knew. Boy this was all our dreams arriving at once, a deluge of intel we could only in our wildest dreams had hoped for.

He had a rat in hell's chance that his information would result in him being granted witness protection, he was heading for a fate to be decided by the full might of the United States of America's judicial system and a place guaranteed in the Cuban sun.

Presumably extradition would be requested from the Haitian Government, or was that a naive assumption, maybe he would just be bundled onto a plane and secreted out of the country. So be it, whatever his future held, I had absolutely zero sympathy with this piece of human excrement.

Wrapping up the interrogation, still leaving many unanswered questions, the interrogator thanked Ramirez and vacated the room.

Joining us in the adjacent room, we awaited his take on what had just taken place and patiently listened to his synopsis of the situation at hand.

On his no doubt expert analysis it was decided to let Ramirez reflect on his candid sharing of information. Basically, to let him sweat in his own juices, whilst the intel he had so easily imparted would start to be analysed and checked thoroughly against existing intelligence.

During this meeting we were informed that the carnage we'd left behind at the former coffee plantation had been "cleaned up." I took that to mean the bodies had been disposed of and all evidence of the gunfight removed, boy they didn't hang around.

Our fear that reinforcements would be sent was proved correct, just a further four, three of which were taken out and the fourth taken prisoner. Another high profile trafficker apparently, wow we certainly had unearthed a seam of these awful characters.

At this point William joined us, without preamble he took over the meeting, he looked serious, and he dove straight in to explain our current situation and the plan going forward. This honourable man had gone completely out on a limb for us right from the beginning, but had we played on his friendship with Christian and his father too heavily, taken advantage of it? Were these friendships' going to be tested to the limit now? These thoughts swirled around my head, for goodness sake I told myself, just listen to what the man had to tell us, before prematurely jumping to conclusions and trying to pre-empt what he had to say.

"My team and I are keeping a lid on this whole thing, thank God, but we've intercepted chatter that strongly indicates a few cages have been rattled to say the least, the corruption goes deeper than you would ever believe possible, and their tentacles are entrenched in the upper echelons of governments of many countries. But this current administration is doing more to try to and eradicate the scourge of human trafficking, drug and arms running than I personally have ever known. That said, the heat is on to wrap this up asap. I'm not privy to all that's going down, but suffice to say on a need to know basis, there are joint ventures in the pipeline to step up the war on trafficking and we don't want you guys caught in the middle of it. But you so deserve to see this part of the jigsaw to fruition, for having the balls and strength of your convictions to even contemplate what you bravely embarked on. For now, I suggest you get some down time, clear your heads and be ready for short notice to be a part of the next phase."

I couldn't quite catch what William said next, but I was pretty certain he'd mumbled "and may God have mercy on our souls" under his breath. Odd didn't begin to cover that statement if I'd heard it correctly. I thought perhaps I'd misheard him. Not dwelling further as I dearly wanted to use what time we had left to reconnect with the children and make contact with my husband.

The former was a joy to behold, and to be reunited with my little bird an utter delight. The embassy staff had worked wonders, the children had been bathed and dressed in fresh clothing and were now engrossed in watching a movie, one I recollected my own children had watched many times.

The one where mice are magically turned into horses, a pumpkin into a carriage and where the search to find the rightful owner of a glass slipper is launched by a handsome prince, a classic.

In the short time we had been back at the Embassy, with gentle urging the children had begun to share details of their backgrounds. They had all been placed without exception by relatives into an orphanage, these relatives unable to care for them, had taken the only course on offer, other than let them fend for themselves on the dangerous streets of Port Au Prince.

With child poverty so prevalent we knew many orphanages had been opened under the guise of philanthropy but tragically with much darker intentions. Not all, many were genuine, alas not the one these children had been placed in. It would now be closely watched, that much we were told.

The latter would prove a little harder, I would have to choose my words carefully. I'd been instructed to use an Embassy telephone, something about the line being scrambled said to me as I was led to a private room.

Taking a deep breath, I dialled Steve's mobile phone number. He answered on the second ring, "Darling, it's me Julia, are you home, can you talk? He replied in the affirmative to both questions. Before I could go further he beat me to it, "just tell me you're ok, I've been worried bloody sick, when are you coming home?"

I replied absolutely fine to the first question and that I had no idea to the second, the line went quiet, prompting me to ask if he was still there. He was, without waiting for him to speak further I gave a brief rundown on what had happened, carefully omitting any mention of guns, Krav Maga and how extremely dangerous the situation had been.

Either falling for my subterfuge or choosing to not talk about it, he seemed content that at least I was in one piece and safe. I added that there were loose ends that had to be tied up, that I didn't know how long it would take or when I would be able to make contact again.

Quickly segueing from my situation, I asked how Jacob, Ethan and Lucy were, had he heard from them, how were the animals, work, everything to steer the conversation away from me. It worked, everyone and everything was good.

Not giving him a chance to question me further I wound up our conversation with a plea to give my love to all concerned, that I loved him deeply, missed him, and that I would be home before too long.

Relief washed over me, like a warm shower, I'd made contact albeit brief, but at least Steve knew I was safe and well. I could fill in the blanks once I was at home, face to face.

As I came out of the room, Christian was waiting, leaning against the wall opposite the door. "How did that conversation go down?" he asked.

"Not one of the best we've ever had," I replied honestly.

Saying nothing more on the subject he grabbed my arm and informed me that a late lunch had been set up for us all, and the magic word wine was mentioned, that added a spring to my step, I really, really could do with a glass or maybe two.

Entering the room I was delighted to see Robert sitting at the table, along with David, Raul, Daniel, William and the guy who had carried out the interview with Ramirez, I couldn't recall his name, and two others whom I didn't recognise.

William gestured to the two as yet unknown guys to introduce themselves, the first identified himself as Erik King. He began a brief but detailed rundown of why he was here, he owned and operated a private security firm, a worldwide covert operation, working with governments under the radar, basically "black ops". Operating in the murky world of hostage rescue, hunting down international terrorists and private protection for anything from Russian Oligarchs to Saudi Princes, to much more in between, although he didn't elaborate on the much, more in between. No reason for why he was here, that would come later.

I was intrigued as to what role he would play, surely his particular services were a world away from what we had become embroiled in. I had no time to ponder further as the second guy was on his feet and starting to introduce himself.

Right, so this guy was known as Carter Payne, employed by Erik King, he ran operations on the ground, briefly touching on his background in the US Military and the NSA before handing back to King.

Now for the meat on the bones so to speak. Employed by the US Government to hunt down in conjunction with US military forces the drug cartels that wreaked so much destruction on American society and their paid henchmen, the incredibly violent and merciless MS 13 gang members.

It was an ongoing all out war to the death, and spanned several South American countries right on through to mainland USA via the Caribbean. Which is where we came into the picture, the part we had played in this becoming clearer by the minute.

Although miniscule in the grand overall scheme, our capture of Luis Ramirez had in fact been fortuitous in more ways than one. He may only be a cog in the monumental wheel of the drug/human trafficking trade, but he had deep connections to the recipients of his sick dealings.

Given leave by the US Government to pursue the Ramirez angle, and you had the reason for King and Payne's presence in a dining room of the US Embassy in Haiti.

This was all well above my pay grade, so I just sat and listened to the ensuing questions posed to the newcomers.

Daniel was the first to dive in, eager to know how they had been alerted to us, the response raised more questions than the simple answer of "there are forces at work that see all, hear all and know all," shutting down that particular line of questioning immediately.

It appeared to me that we were diving deeper down the 'rabbit hole', a hole of monumental proportions, encompassing so much misery and suffering. I just, in all honesty wanted so badly to put my hands over my ears and not be privy to such profound evil.

But I was here on my own volition, indeed I was the reason we were all here, but never in my wildest nightmares had I envisioned this.

Reaching for my wine glass, Robert sitting to my left, second guessed me and poured a healthy serving. I in turn, took a large mouthful before offering my thanks. Oh it tasted like nectar to the God's on my tongue, never before had I quite so appreciated it, feeling its effects as the alcoholic warmth spread through my body.

Robert whispered a few words, "These are great guys to have on our side, keep the faith and relax my dear."

King added that he and Payne would be taking their turn at interrogating Ramirez as they heavily suspected he was withholding further vital intel, "We are in absolutely no doubt, this dude knows where the bodies are buried metaphorically speaking, and he can lead us to them, you guys came in at a very opportune time, we knew he had moved his operations from narcotics to human trafficking, but he covered his tracks well."

As we ate lunch, King and Payne filled in some of the gaps I definitely had with regards to how and where the supply chain of adults and children were satisfied. With political unrest and poverty rife in South America it was sickeningly easy to procure cargo. Promising the adults a better life in the North, they were even willing to pay for their own passage, a double whammy for the traffickers. Little did these tragic people know what awaited them.

Many of them had children, they would be forcibly separated later. Most of the children however were sourced from unscrupulous orphanages, where palms would be handsomely greased to turn a blind eye, street children were easy prey too.

Once at the borders any adults without children would be instructed to take the unaccompanied minors through with them, claiming them as their own. Thus satisfying the authorities and the media would of course be on hand to provide the necessary heart breaking film footage of these human caravans, playing their part in the subterfuge, for the unsuspecting world to see. All the while this was happening with the full glare of publicity, many would also cross at remote parts of the border.

Added to this and something I was totally ignorant of was the use of underground tunnels, from the border with Mexico right up to and including Arizona. These tunnels were originally dug and used by the drug traffickers and arms were smuggled too.

In the depths of my memory I remembered reading somewhere about something called Operation Fast and Furious which was an illicit gun running mob, so I was aware of gun running.

Not content with having all this at their disposal the traffickers also used the sea for their movement of human misery. The Caribbean was perfectly situated for this, given its relatively close proximity to mainland USA. Add to the mix the fact that islands like Haiti were poverty stricken, corrupt and chaotic, it was a smorgasbord for these parasites to feast on.

In a little over an hour I had learned so much. The twelve children we had rescued were but a drop in the ocean, but on the positive side these children were now safe and there were mighty powers at work to ruthlessly track down and eliminate the modern day slave trade known as human trafficking.

After lunch King and Payne made their way for a "chat" with Ramirez, whilst we were asked to stay in the room and await their return.

The time waiting was spent with William asking us for a debriefing of what had transpired at the coffee plantation. Although officially of course it never happened, William still wanted a full run down of the course of events, which had led to quite a body count and twelve rescued children and the capture of Ramirez.

He listened intently not commenting until we had finished. "Well, on a wing and prayer you guys pulled it off, I'd say you were fucking lucky and I salute all of you and I feel honoured to have played my part, it might still cost me my position, but hey I've had a good run so far, without too much catching up with me."

His candour was refreshing and not a little surprising, but why oh why did I have the innate feeling the jovial tone of his voice hadn't quite reached his eyes. He then turned to me and laid out what he had planned for the conclusion of my role in this saga.

Officially I was still in the Dominican Republic, having crossed over on false papers, ditto for Christian.

Depending on what transpired with King and Payne, William ultimately wanted to make sure we were safely out of Haiti, back in the Dominican Republic where we would be able to take flights home. So he had made tentative arrangements to have Christian and I driven back over the border when it was needed.

It sounded so final, I'd known in my heart of hearts that we wouldn't ever be able to save all the children in one go, but I felt in my bones that the tide was turning, for the good.

As events unfolded with the return of King and Payne, it appeared my departure from Haiti would be delayed.

Feelings of euphoria and trepidation fought with each other, racing through my brain with equal measure. Like a rollercoaster going higher, then the drop from the top.

By now it was late afternoon and plans were being made at lightning speed, following on from what had been further gleaned from Ramirez. By fair means or foul, not one of us asked, in truth we didn't give a shit if they'd had his balls in a vice. He'd spilled his guts and more.

In a nutshell, the children we had rescued were destined to be transferred by boat, to a privately owned island. A paradise playground for a well connected billionaire with a predilection for young children. Far, far away from prying eyes or questions asked. No pesky neighbours to worry about or nosy investigative reporters to evade, or law enforcement either.

As this new information was being imparted to us the hairs on the back of my neck began to rise. That primal response which without fail had always alerted me to some sixth sense, my stomach began to churn too.

Frantically trying to search the recesses of my memory for why my subconscious would react so intently to this latest revelation when it hit me like a speeding juggernaut and I was filled with dread.

I took a furtive glance at Christian, he held my eye and in that split second he knew I'd remembered that conversation we'd had not that long ago. When he'd casually mentioned his incredibly wealthy in-laws owned a private island in the Caribbean!.

Not missing a trick, King had witnessed the silent but telling eye contact Christian and I had made with each other, and in a heartbeat calmly turned his attention to Christian.

"It's standard procedure for us to carry out background checks on anyone we decide can be privy to our intelligence sharing and operations, and some pretty interesting and situation relevant stuff came back regarding your wife's family. Shall I go further or would you prefer to inform the room?"

The tension was almost tangible as Christian rose to his feet. "OK, it's not a secret that my wife Candace's parents are stinking rich and just happen to own a small island in the Caribbean, and yes I've visited the place several times, but that doesn't make them paid up members of some sick and twisted club that preys on young kids, does it?"

King went back at Christian "In our line of business rarely do we believe in coincidences, that's not to say we doubt you in the slightest, your check came back practically squeaky clean, apart from some pot smoking in college that your Father made disappear, but the same can't be said for your wife's parents and their shall we say social circle!"

He went further, "When you were on the island, can you recall the level of security, surveillance etc, we're getting some pretty good satellite imagery and we have the original architects plans, but there aren't too many checks made once building plans are submitted and granted. Palms are greased and it's pretty much carte blanche from then onwards. We do know with utmost certainty that there are tunnels beneath the main building, leading to subsequent outer buildings and then onto the beach area and possibly linkage to nearby islands. Did you ever use these subterranean passageways?"

Christian replied with genuine shock in his voice "No way Man, I did not know of any goddam tunnels. As for security, there were always armed guards patrolling the perimeter and cameras everywhere, which freaked me out, as the joke was, if we even farted they'd know about it. But you know I took that with a grain of salt, but with hindsight the fuckers were probably watching everything we did. Before you ask, I mentioned this to Julia only recently that at times things felt and looked strange, odd even. I just assumed they were all a bunch of masons' and the island was like the ultimate lodge or whatever their terminology is. I made it clear from the outset I wasn't interested in weird handshakes and all their crap. I literally went there to play tennis, scuba dive and generally chillout, and I'd like to add I only visited the place three times."

It was as if the rest of us weren't in the room, as the conversation just boomeranged between King and Christian. Christian genuinely did not know of these tunnels nor trafficked children and that was abundantly clear to all of us in the room, especially me, my dear friend was not capable of being a part of all this evil, absolutely not. I would willingly stake my life on it.

Something else was becoming abundantly clear too, that we were only being told a fraction of what was taking place behind the scenes. Of course I understood why, these monsters had infiltrated every layer of public life and government, their wicked web spun like gossamer through every strata. Money bought loyalty and silence.

Realising Christian could provide no valuable information, King stepped the meeting up a few gears and began to unveil the plans for the next stage. We weren't asked to leave the room, leaving me to surmise that we would all be allowed to take part in it, that's what I was praying for.

Once again, we were using the miracle that is satellite imagery, but this time we had the luxury of viewing it on a large screen. No huddling around the laptop, it enabled us to sit back and really digest the pictures being downloaded.

During the next thirty minutes, along with details of the island, we learned that the island was wholly owned and registered to a Mr & Mrs Jerome Clay the III, (Candace's parents) of Connecticut USA. Old money made from the usual sources of railroads and newspapers, the dynasty starting in the late nineteenth century, surviving the Great Depression, diversifying into pharmaceuticals in the fifties to be one of the wealthiest families stateside.

King and Payne had certainly left no stone unturned, building an in-depth picture of the Clay family. They counted many Senators and Congressmen as close friends, along with a good helping of international politicians, film stars, philanthropic billionaires and even several European royals to boot.

Christian looked shocked at the mention of royals, adding that Candace had been around the glitterati all her life and usually liked to name drop, but had never mentioned a royal one.

Back to the island. The main island was forty miles in circumference and known as St. Lucy. It had a landing strip for aircraft, big enough for a commercial airliner to land, a landing pad for helicopters and a sizeable dock for boats.

We were able to clearly see the main house, which was single storey, several much smaller buildings which Christian identified as guest suites and a gymnasium. Much further from the main house was the staff residence. There were other buildings scattered around the island too, bloody hell, all this for one family's holiday retreat!.

Next came the logistics, St. Lucy was situated approximately 420 nautical miles from Port Au Prince, quite a trip. Calculating at an average speed of twenty knots, it would take us around eighteen hours to reach our destination.

The majority of the trip would be undertaken by a US Coastguard Cutter, then the remainder by RIB (rigid inflatable boat). If I hadn't understood the lengths being taken to tackle and rid the world of human trafficking I truly did now. Huge resources were being made available, seemingly at short notice, but something didn't sit right with me, feeling like a student in class I raised my arm to ask a question.

"This is all just incredible and I'm finding it difficult to express my depth of gratitude, however I have to ask how come this has all been organised so expediently and it appears with unlimited funds?".

King with a rock hard glare replied "I explained previously that Ramirez was on our radar, and you guys did the legwork for us. We knew he was trafficking kids to the elite and beyond, we had several islands under surveillance but without a concrete link, we wouldn't have the green light for go. Ramirez singing like a canary to save his ass, gave us the link we needed, so it's a plan that's been in the making for a while, he was the catalyst for all systems go. As for funding, that's on a need-to-know basis and I'll be as polite as possible ma'am, you don't need to know."

I replied, "Thank you Mr King, your candour is much appreciated, but I must ask a further question. How come we," and I gestured to my band of brothers, "are being allowed to be privy to all this and even more so permitted to join the trip to the island?"

"Well you have William to thank for it, he thought you guys deserved to be included, especially you Julia, you kinda kicked this whole thing off. Christian you could prove invaluable too, Daniel and Raul you both have put your careers and safety on the line, to do the right thing and lastly David, well you will always be a brother in arms," King replied.

Satisfied and quite chuffed with King's answer I relaxed back in my chair, mouthing a silent thank you to William as I did so.

The plan came together rapidly, but with the expertise and experience of King and Payne I wasn't at all surprised, added to that the fact that most of it had been in the works before we came along, it all fell into place smoothly.

Although there were to be strict caveats to our being allowed to join this operation, basically we would not be allowed anywhere near the initial incursion, this would be carried out by highly trained military personnel. They would be wearing body cameras, which would relay the whole operation back to the ship, at anchor just two miles from St. Lucy.

Using RIB's to reach the shore, they would surround and secure the island. Then the most delicate part would commence, the part where Ramirez would be used, with several military guys posing as his cohorts. Payne emphasised his confidence that Ramirez wouldn't attempt to compromise the mission, as he was well aware he'd be a "dead man walking" if he tried.

Payne revealed that the clean-up of the coffee plantation had been so thorough there had been no intercepted communications of alarm further down the trafficking chain. This enabled them to use Ramirez, and under close control, he'd been communicating with Clay's people as if he were still a free man at large to deliver his goods. It had worked perfectly, the net was closing in.

Ramirez would then demand to meet Clay face to face, under the guise that there was so much heat going down the price for the cargo had gone up. Once he engaged Clay in a conversation confirming his involvement in the trafficking of children to his island, the green light for go would be given, all hell would break loose.

Once everything was contained, then Christian, David, Raul, Daniel and I would be transferred to the island, to witness the vile scum under arrest. That was to be the ultimate reward for the part we had played.

I wanted to pinch myself hard as it all seemed so surreal, as if I were in a fast, action-packed dream, a dream so farfetched it could only be taking place in the realms of a deep sleep or indeed a Hollywood movie.

Now to put it all into action, to roll the dice and see how they fall.

Chapter 24

The Island
When the Storm has swept by, the wicked are gone, but the righteous stand firm forever.
Proverbs 10.25

The operation had to be carried out with the cover of darkness, meaning we would depart the Embassy in the early hours of the morning.

Quietly leaving the compound at 2 a.m., we travelled further up the coast to a secluded beach, there waiting for us the transport to the Coastguard cutter. Kitted out in life jackets we climbed aboard and the engine sprang to life and we were off.

Within ten minutes or so the cutter came into view, and in no time we were scrambling up ropes thrown over the side, welcome arms assisted me onto its deck.

As all the team were successfully transferred, I heard the instruction to pull anchor and set sail, we set off into the night, I glanced heavenward to see a tableau of stars in a stunningly clear night, like sentinels accompanying us on our journey.

Leading us down a flight of stairs to a large area that I can only describe as a general meeting area for the crew, a uniformed officer told us to wait there and the Captain would be joining us shortly.

I heard him before well before I saw him, a booming voice barking orders as he made his way to us. A great bear of a man, standing there in his pristine uniform, I instantly had an overwhelming feeling of trust and security in Captain Dwight Pendleton.

After welcoming us aboard his boat, he dived straight into the plan at hand. We would be cruising at an average speed of twenty knots, the waters were calm and he foresaw nothing that would or could cause delay. Our estimated time of arrival would be approximately 20.00 hundred hours, placing us five nautical miles from the island of St. Lucy. Weighing anchor, he would await instructions to launch the rapid inflatables.

He indicated toward a large screen that had been set up and explained this would be where the filmed footage of the rendezvous will be relayed and observed by those remaining onboard. He was aware that once the island was secured and incriminating footage obtained, then further inflatables were to be launched to ferry us to the island.

Captain Pendleton also informed the gathered group that they were fully equipped and had ample room for hostiles to be held and transported to wherever it was deemed they would be taken to. They were to be treated as enemies of the state and the full might of the law implemented against them, adding further his own personal disgust at human traffickers and the evil bastards that purchased their goods. "We're going to try our damndest to assist you in rounding this filth up and lock their sorry asses away."

Well not one of us would disagree with that speech, indeed this may well be just an infinitesimal part of the worldwide trafficking cartels, but plenty was being primed and aimed to cut one head off the Hydra. The rest would fall like dominoes hopefully.

Gratefully accepting the offer of bunk beds as Captain Pendleton advised we get some "shut eye for a few hours" Christian, Raul, Daniel and I duly followed a young officer to the sleeping quarters.

I noticed David hung back with King and Payne, not thinking too much of it as I was beginning to feel weary and the thought of a bunk for a few hours was just too inviting.

Christian ever the gentleman offered me the bottom bunk, to which I eagerly clambered into, mumbling my thanks as I did so. Raul and Daniel followed suit.

Once comfortably ensconced in our little cocoons, sleep beckoned, however Christian had other ideas and began whispering, loud enough for Raul and Daniel to hear too.

"Guys, I hope you believed me when I said I knew nothing of what was going on at St. Lucy's, man I had no idea and I was just as shocked as you all were. They sure as hell had me fooled."

Practically in unison Raul, Daniel and I assured Christian that we had no doubts at all in him and he was stupid to even think that.

My friend of so many years was a kind and gentle soul, without an ounce of malice of that I was more than certain and anyway my treasured grandmother would have known, her sixth sense alerted her to people of dubious character. I never knew her to be wrong in her judgement, such a wise soul.

Having done our job of comforting my friend, silence descended and sleep beckoned. Clearing my mind I began to drift off to the land of slumber. I felt inordinately relaxed and at one with myself, the calm before the storm came to my mind. However my feeling of contentment didn't last very long!.

They hadn't come to me for several days now, when I'd had the chance to rest it had been without the disturbance of my ethereal companions. I'd reasoned to myself that they must be content with the outcome of the rescue mission at the coffee plantation.

I was so very wrong in my assumption, as always it happened in that twilight space between conscientiousness and sleep, when my mind was most relaxed and receptive to messages from another realm.

Their beautiful, angelic yet mournful faces began to flood my mind and their voices followed.

"Manman nou di nou mesi pou sove timoun yo" another voice joined in "Gen danje devan, ou te paye anvan, pou fwa sa yo, nou tout ki bo kote ou, pou gide ak pwoteje ou."

As quickly as they had appeared they were gone, back into the ether. I struggled to wake, my mind drowsy, and yet aware that I was mumbling incoherently.

As I fought to come back to reality I felt a hand on my forehead and heard voices urging me to wake up.

Slowly opening my eyes and desperately trying to focus, I realised it was Raul touching me and soothing me, with Daniel and Christian, kneeling on the ground behind him.

I had to get out from the bunk, claustrophobia and confusion were engulfing me, taking deep, steadying breaths I swung my legs out first, then managed to raise to myself on one arm.

"They came back to me, but I can't recall what they said, oh my God I can't remember, there were too many words, but I think it was a warning."

Raul intervened "Julia, you were repeating their words in your sleep, we got them don't stress yourself".

I grabbed hold of his hands and pleaded with him to tell me, "The first sentence was Mother we give thanks for saving the children, the second is more troubling. It was there is danger ahead, you have been spared before, for this time, we are all around you, to guide and protect you."

I looked at the three of them kneeling in front of me, once again wide awake and in control of my faculties and spoke clearly "Raul, repeat that second message again, I get the warning of danger but the rest is freaking me out."

Raul obliged me and repeated the sentence and I replied, "I've been spared before, what the hell does that mean ?" I implored. Three blank faces just stared back at me.

"Perhaps it will all be explained to you one day" Daniel added and carried on talking "I am concerned at the danger ahead warning, we must keep our wits about us at all times my friends'."

Indeed, they were wise words from Daniel, but my brain was in overdrive, searching for an answer to how I'd been saved before for this time. Try as I might I couldn't find one, racking the recesses of my memory to no avail.

Feeling guilty at interrupting their much needed rest I urged the guys to go back to sleep, knowing that was beyond me for now. After they'd settled back in their bunks I ventured back on deck, hoping the warm breeze and the motion of the boat ploughing through the sea would soothe my anxious state of mind.

I stood motionless on the deck and let the warm breeze caress and soothe my troubled soul, I'd always loved the sea, had an affinity with it from a very young age, never fearful of its immense power, just respect for its majesty.

Dawn was beginning to break and with it the myriad of stunning colours, marvelling at the earth's ability to morph from the night's blackness to a crescendo of brightness, the golden rays hopefully lighting our path with good speed, calm seas and the armour of our holy God for protection against any dangers we may face.

It did the trick, I began to feel the calmness I'd felt before drifting off to sleep, nodding at the sailor on duty, I made my way back to my bunk. The guys were all sound asleep, settling myself down, sleep descended and this time it was uninterrupted and untroubled.

Stirring, I had no idea what the time was, how long I had slept. Noticing the other bunks were empty, I made my way back to the meeting area. It turned out I'd managed to rest for several hours, unbelievable, but I felt so much better for it.

Acknowledging my entrance Christian beckoned for me to join them at a table they were all sitting at, David included. Passing me a large mug of coffee which I gratefully accepted, I thanked them for letting me sleep in.

I sat quietly savouring the coffee, whilst they resumed their conversation.

I'd missed an update from King and Captain Pendleton. The latter confirming we were on course with no delays and would arrive on schedule. The former advising that intel had been received that Mr and Mrs Clay were both in residence on St. Lucy and Ramirez was fully primed as to his role in the take down of the Clays.

Short and sweet but straight to the point, now we would sit out the rest of the voyage, wait at anchor until 22.00 hundred hours when the inflatables would be launched to take Ramirez and the others to the island…

We had hours to kill before the action started, I so wanted to make contact with my family at home, but any and all outside contact was forbidden, understandable but frustrating.

The intervening hours were spent either on deck, watching pods of dolphins perform their acrobatics on the water or below deck playing cards and genuinely trying to be as relaxed as possible. But we were all silently eager for the dice to be rolled and justice served.

The clock on the wall showed 21.30 hours. We were all congregated once again in the meeting area, an air of anticipation palpable and felt by us all I was sure. The screen loomed large in the room and would soon come to life bringing us a birds eye view of the meeting between Ramirez and Clay.

The first team responsible for securing the perimeter of the island and buildings had already departed the boat. We neither saw them leave or were introduced to these shadowy figures, who had been sequestered well away from us, their identities forever secret. These brave unknown warriors who time and again risked their lives, so we can live ours in peace and safety.

Every scenario had been thought of, even down to the inflatable that would be used by Ramirez. This would be a civilian craft, there must be nothing that could theoretically lead to suspicion being roused. This was the most delicate part of the operation and if anything went awry this early on it would only lead to disaster and the threat of an aborted mission.

Adding to the mix was Clay being alerted to the fact he was under suspicion and being shadowed. In turn this would lead to the whole vile network knowing they had been rumbled, they would scurry like rats to their bolt holes, never facing the full wrath of the law for their depravities and crimes against children/humanity.

We weren't privy to Ramirez's departure, only that King and Payne would lead the sortie posing as his accomplices, with four extra men as their backup.

It seemed like an eternity before the clock registered time for the green light for go. In unison, we all fell silent, straightening in our seats and awaited the screen to come to life. The anticipation and dare I say, it was tangible, like an undetectable electric current flowing through everyone present. I could only compare it to watching a movie where the President was in the situation room, waiting for events to be relayed to him.

The lights were dimmed in readiness and hey presto the screen came to life. Although darkness had long since descended, the miracle of technology showed us the scene in the inflatable. All present had body cams apart from Ramirez who was wearing an eavesdropping wire.

Only one camera was at present relaying back to base, but it was enough for us to see their steady journey to St. Lucy. The screen was capable of being split into six boxes, thus enabling live feeds from various parts of the island.

Other boxes on the screen began relaying video feeds, these were from the scouting crew, now confirming they were in place and all combatants neutralised. I took this to mean that the island's security personnel had been dealt with, meaning they were dead.

I sat between Christian and Raul and I couldn't help but grab their hands as the tension mounted. King as Beta team leader could be heard stating they were coming into the dock area and would be going silent until the rendezvous.

By this time my heart literally felt as though it were lodged in my throat, such was the suspense, and you could have heard a pin drop in what was now being called the "situation room."

Captain Pendleton was also seated, he was in a deep and hushed conversation with several of his officers and three others. I would describe these individuals as civilian personnel, as they weren't in uniform, I hadn't seen them before and we hadn't been introduced, more three letter agency guys no doubt.

The team in the inflatable were now alongside the wooden docking pier, after tying it up they quickly mounted the ladder. They began walking along the walkway towards the island, it was well lit with lights on each of the wooden posts, so synonymous of beachside hotels.

Nearing the end of the walkway King nudged Ramirez to the front of the group, keeping up the appearance that Ramirez was the one in control.

Waiting for them were several golf carts, no doubt to ferry them to the main building. Audio kicked into life and we could hear Ramirez remonstrating with Clay's people.

The plan was for the liaison with Clay to be held on the dock. Out in the open, less chance for the bad guys to have cover. Shit it was going awry already.

We were able to clearly hear Ramirez, keeping his cool, and arrogantly stating "that if the boss wanted to talk money and cargo he would get his fucking ass down here now."

All eyes were firmly on the screen, watching the drama unfold. King introducing himself as Ramirez's partner quickly took control. "That's not a problem, lead the way." Crisis averted, I let out the breath I'd subconsciously held in, they'd obviously planned for every scenario, have faith Julia I said to myself, these guys are the best of the best. Balls of steel came to my mind, indeed balls of steel.

King kept close to Ramirez, travelling in the same cart, with his back up men travelling behind. Silence fell over the airwaves, the only sound coming from the vehicles. A short time later they pulled up outside the main house, a single storey, whitewashed yet innately elegant building.

Exiting the golf carts and standing to face the house, the bodycam worn by King afforded us a good view of the main entrance. There were four large steps leading up to it, with a porch that wrapped around the whole building, this we already knew from the satellite imagery seen previously.

Standing at the top of these steps was none other than Jerome Clay the third himself, surrounded by four of his own henchmen. He stood there for several moments, before descending the steps to join the group now all assembled, Ramirez, King and their four backups.

Many things struck me at this precise moment, but the most prominent was Clay's demeanour. Relaxed, calm almost jovial, and yet this monster was about to bargain for children's lives.

Shaking hands with Ramirez, he turned his attention to King, the timbre of his voice belied his body language as his voice, laced with menace could be heard "I don't appreciate unknowns coming to my island to conduct business, who are you and why are you here?"

Cool, aloof and just as menacing King retorted, "I don't appreciate having to travel halfway across the Caribbean to barter with a sick old bastard, when the heat is on, the goddam feds are everywhere, so you either pay what we're asking or we just turn around and leave. There's plenty that are willing to pay for what we have."

Somewhat placated, but oozing with arrogance Clay came back at King, "My tastes are none of your business and you're equally as sick for trading the kids in the first place. But as this maybe the last shipment for some time, I'm willing to pay $2,000 a kid. On the usual terms, cash on delivery once they've been inspected." And as simple as that Clay had been entrapped and the evidence captured, it was almost too easy. Clay had fallen for it, hook, line and sinker.

The bile rose in my throat and the feeling of revulsion overwhelmed me at Clay's words. I swear down that had it been me standing in front of him and I had a gun, I would've shot him dead. The world would be a far better place without this evil creature in it, swift justice meted out to a demon.

Within seconds the action commenced. Drawing their guns, King, Payne and the four men accompanying them aimed their weaponry on Clay and his men, but they weren't going down without a fight. Instantaneously reaching for their guns, but they weren't quick enough. Silencers meant no sound was emitted, but the head shots were rapid and deadly.

All four taken out in swift succession. As they fell to the ground, Clay with an agility belying his years turned to run. But he wasn't quite quick enough, and a blow to his head from the butt of King's gun rendered him unconscious, kneeling down beside him King roughly pulled his arms behind his back and cable tied them together. Clay they wanted alive, to face his time in court and hopefully spend the rest of his life behind bars.

Leaving him trussed up like a turkey at Thanksgiving, King and his men began to move the four dead bodies out of sight behind thick bushes that surrounded the veranda, leaving no trace of the carnage that had just taken place.

What took place next had me reaching forward in my seat, incredulous. Ramirez seizing the opportunity of King and his men's attention being taken with clearing up, he bent to grab one of Clay's dead henchman's guns left on the ground. But he was no match for these guys, they must have anticipated him making such a move, as with lethal speed Payne reached him, striking him hard on the head, he slumped to the ground, knocked out stone cold, he too was then trussed up with cable ties.

I wasn't the only one in the situation room to let out an audible sigh of relief, glancing around at those gathered, the tension was evident. By no means was this over yet, and I had the most awful feeling of déjà-vu, silently remonstrating with myself to think objectively and not give way to my imagination.

One man was left behind to stand guard over the captives, whilst the rest entered the main house. From the footage being relayed back to us I could see a huge entrance hall, lit by an enormous crystal chandelier, under it stood a round table with the most stunning floral arrangement sat atop it, just simply beautiful. Dark wooden floors were gleaming in the light.

We were being given a panoramic view on screen, enabling us to see many doors leading from the hall and directly beyond the table was a wide entrance with steps down to an imposing open plan lounge area. Again, this room was well lit, but eerily devoid of any signs of life.

The whole area was deserted, which was at odds with the intel that had been received, but before I could ponder further on the strange situation at hand, the sound of gunfire could be heard, ricocheting around the entrance hall.

The dreaded words that none of us wanted to hear came through loud and clear "man down". As we watched the ensuing gun fight from the safety of the cutter, the footage relayed back to us showed an open door through which the gunman had unexpectedly entered the hall.

Communicating between themselves, King and his team of commandos turned their guns on the assailant and took him down with bullets to the head and torso. Brains and blood were sprayed onto the whitewashed walls, as he fell to the ground, the shots that entered cleanly through his chest had wreaked massive damage upon exiting his back.

Attention now was on our injured man, dropping to his knees Payne could be clearly heard and seen giving medical attention and summoning the second team who had secured the perimeter of the island to get themselves to the main building asap.

His Kevlar vest had saved the injured man from a bullet fired at his chest, but a bullet had hit him in the upper thigh and the blood loss looked bad, really bad. Calmly applying a tourniquet to stem the bleeding and talking to the injured man "stay with me Baker, stay awake, stay with me man."

As Payne was administering medical aid, the others were checking the whole of the ground floor and we could hear "room clear" coming through their headsets as they methodically made their way from room to room.

Within minutes several members of the second team had arrived at the house, from their bodycams we witnessed one of them remove his backpack, delve into it, kneel and assist Payne with the injured man.

Payne's voice came through loud and clear after several minutes, "Captain Pendleton Sir, we've stemmed the bleeding, but we need an evac team here asap."

Pendleton responded immediately, rising to his feet he answered Payne, "Evac team ready to go, I'll give the order to launch, switch to their frequency and liaise directly, and thank God you saved him, well done."

My attention had been solely on the conversation between Payne and Captain Pendleton, my concern for the injured man paramount in my mind. But David had obviously managed to observe and digest all the feeds coming back to us from the island.

He was animatedly drawing attention to the pictures being relayed back to us from one of the rooms being searched and wasted no time in letting us know what had been found. "That's how the bastard went undetected, what's the betting this is the entrance to the tunnels" as I began following his direction, in real time, with the wonders of modern technology at our fingertips, and with a front row seat, we one and all saw a large wooden door, positioned next to a grand fireplace, (when would you require a fireplace in the Caribbean) open, and the bodycam wearer enter the dark recess beyond it.

Indeed, this appeared to be the beginning of the labyrinth of tunnels we knew existed in the bowels of the island. This might answer the question uppermost in all our minds as to why there was an obvious lack of human presence in the main house. The rats had scattered, using their hidden escape route, to evade their impending capture.

King, notified of this discovery began to issue orders and directions. This was pure poetry in motion, ordering the remainder of the second back up team to stay in their positions around the circumference of the island, he handpicked several of his men to follow him down this freshly discovered rabbit hole.

The atmosphere in the control room was electric, pulsating with anticipation, an electric current joining all of us in unison, on one hand terrified of what might be revealed, but on the other, wanting corroboration of what we had all suspected, that this island and its heinous secrets would justify our quest for rescuing the children whose only existence was to serve the monsters that preyed upon them.

All the while we sat watching events on the island unfold, the ship's crew were so very attentive, the coffee flowed, food offered and our general well-being pandered to. The only thing we unanimously agreed on accepting was coffee, although we didn't need caffeine to keep us awake, it helped nonetheless.

Word came back to us that the injured man was back on board and receiving the very best of medical care. Such an immense relief, I honestly don't know how I would have coped with his death, as it would be fairly and squarely on my shoulders would it not? Yet another heartfelt prayer of thanks was sent heavenward.

At this rate I would be spending goodness knows how long in eternal gratitude to my Lord God, him whom I turn to in times of need but regrettably forget in the good times. I made a promise to myself to never be so shallow ever again.

What transpired in the ensuing hours will forever be engraved in my memory, as visible as a tattoo, inked on my body as a future reminder of past events, made manifest with huge faith in having the fortitude, the belief so strongly held, that each and every one of us has the ability to right so many wrongs, if we possess the strength of our convictions. If only we listened to our inner voice, haranguing us to put our collective heads above the parapet, to not be afraid of ridicule or scorn, when we believe we are right.

With their escape route blocked, it didn't take long for Clay's fellow deviants to be rounded up. It was only then that we were summoned to the island to bear witness to the sheer and unimaginable evil that had been allowed to foment, without fear of being uncovered, because wealth and influence can bring with it an armour of protection, aided and abetted by their sheer and breathtaking arrogance.

As we made our way to the island, clouds were gathering in the night sky, covering the tableau of stars that had been so magnificent earlier. Strange as no storms were forecast, but the humidity level was rising, wrapping us all in a cloak of dampness, that precursor so synonymous with the build up to the heavens opening and wreaking down its vengeance on us mere mortals. The scent of rain, heavy in the air, all pervading our senses, ominous and threatening, yet silent in its stealth, like a big cat tracking its prey before unleashing its strength for the final assault.

Waiting for our arrival at the dockside stood two heavily armed men, dressed from head to toe in black, balaclavas disguising their identities, dark sentinels sent to escort us to the main house. I recalled thinking when watching them on the live screen how they reminded me of a time many years ago, when the whole world was privy to the storming of the Iranian Embassy in London.

These dark clad warriors, their identities unknown, yet their bravery unrivalled and our collective gratitude as a nation to them unanimous. Yes, they indeed reminded me of our valiant SAS, fearless, courageous, and thanks to God, they were on our side.

As we travelled by golf carts to the main house, the static electricity from the gathering storm was evident all around us, the electric charges that build up until they are finally released as streams of electrons that create a bolt of lightning, not far off now.

How fitting that our final coup de grace for Clay and his depraved cohorts would be accompanied by a show of Mother Nature's ire, the uncontrollable force of a tempest, to show her rage at the terrible acts carried out on the most innocent of our world, the children. It brought part of Psalm 11:5:6 clearly to my mind "Upon the wicked he shall rain, snares, fire and brimstone and a horrible tempest. So be it, never before had my faith been so strong, nor my reliance on good prevailing over evil.

Entering the main hall with Christian by my side, David, Raul and Daniel directly behind, felt so very weird. Only an hour before we had watched this same room from a screen, now standing in it, I could grasp the sheer size of the floor space, it was huge.

No attempt had been made to remove the body of the gunman, and try as I might to not glance at the corpse, morbid curiosity won out. A crimson tide of blood encircled it, its life fluid seeping out and staining the beautiful mahogany flooring, its metallic scent still detectable in the air.

Glancing away from the body I scanned the surrounding walls and saw the contents of his brain, sprayed on them, I felt no remorse nor revulsion, just an overwhelming sense of ambivalence, or indeed emotional detachment, or perhaps both. Either way I felt no sadness or regret at a life lost.

King and Payne came striding out from one of the doors leading off the main hall, grave expressions on their faces and an urgency in their step. King spoke first.

"Be prepared for what you're going to see, I just hope to God, you've got strong guts. Even my guys who believe me, have seen some bad situations, are emotional, follow me please."

As we filed out of the main hall following King's lead, I instantly recognised the room with the fireplace and the door to the side of it. Payne then started issuing instructions to us and his men.

"Keep to single file down the staircase, once at the bottom, keep going straight past the dungeons, there will be time later to show you what's in there, we just want the captives identified, photographed and their asses hauled back to the ship pronto."

I couldn't help myself. My voice gave life to what was running through my head. "Fucking hell did I just hear dungeons?" My voice rising in shock.

Payne replied quickly, "Yes Ma'am, as the Boss said, be prepared."

No further words were spoken, we silently followed in single file, traversing the room, we crossed the entrance to the staircase.

It was as if we had gone back in time and had found ourselves in a medieval castle, as the staircase was made of stone, as were the walls, our descent being lit by wall sconces, albeit electric and not flame.

Reaching the bottom, I braced myself, determined to keep my line of sight straight ahead and to not look to the sides. I found myself unable to, and my eyes darted from side to side and were met by images straight from some sort of dreadful horror movie.

One in which thick wooden doors, with steel bars set high up in them, held grim secrets and terrors, that from the comfort of your armchair or a movie theatre, you knew weren't real, just Hollywood make-believe. Only now we were walking past such ominous portals in real time.

Taking deep breaths to steady and calm myself, I managed to put one foot in front of the other and keep walking and looking straight ahead.

The long corridor opened out onto a large, well lit, low ceilinged, square room, hewn from rock. As my eyes took in the scene before me, and before my brain could fully digest the images, Christian's voice, loud and incredulous, boomed out and seemed to ricochet around the stone walls, such was the intensity in his tone.

"Candace, please dear God tell me you are not a part of this?"

The raw distress in his voice was visceral, and in it I could feel the struggle to maintain his composure, the anger rising like a dormant volcano, ready to burst forth and spill a raging torrent of red hot molten lava down upon the woman on the floor in front of him.

As the shock reverberated through the whole of my body, the feeling was one of being physically shaken by an unseen entity, then my eyes as if in slow motion moved from my friend to the floor in the centre of the room, there was no mistaking, it was Christian's estranged wife.

Candace was not alone, slowly and in turn I tried to identify the people with her, only now noticing their arms appeared to be bound behind their backs and as with Candace their mouths were gagged.

Confirming to myself the two by Candace's side were her parents was easy, not only had I been a guest at their daughter's wedding, but Jerome Clay had been on screen earlier, although now he appeared to be fully conscious.

As I scanned the others huddled with them, and it took several seconds for the penny of recognition to drop, it hit me hard, as sitting there in the middle of the room was none other than the man who had approached me at the airport in the UK, before I boarded my flight to the Dominican Republic.

He simultaneously locked eyes with me and throwing his head back, then forward, making the universally known gesture of actually spitting at me. I instinctively took a step back, swallowing hard to contain the bile that was rising to the back of my throat.

David quickly noticed my reaction and took hold of my arm. "Jesus Christ, you look like you've seen a ghost."

Stammering, I managed to get the words out, "That's him, the guy who approached me at the airport, but why is he here?"

Before David was able to answer, our attention was diverted to the raised voices of Christian and King. Oh shit, it was kicking off between them, with Christian just inches away from King's face.

"Can you please just take the goddam gag out of her mouth, I need to hear her tell me she isn't a part of all this fucking sick crap."

King came back at Christian. "Please just stand back, calm the fuck down and I will remove the gag."

Somewhat placated Christian stepped back, allowing King to pass and as good as his word King bent over Candace and removed the gag.

I'd always found Candace amiable, impeccably mannered, albeit with an air of aloofness about her, which I'd put down to her silver spooned upbringing. Who was I kidding, she had the whole canteen of silver cutlery in her mouth when she was born!

Hence, I struggled to reconcile the Candace of the past to the vile, venomous bitch of a woman now screeching at her husband, the malice dripping from every word, like acid, stripping any vestige of love and respect left between them. It was truly horrific and heart breaking all at once to be a witness to it.

Gone was the sophisticated and well-polished socialite, in its place a desperate, screeching wreck of a woman, one I no longer recognised.

"You just couldn't keep that fucking nose out, you always were a useless, sanctimonious sack of shit, why the fuck did I ever marry you. I told Daddy you would never tow the fucking line, to join our circle of the enlightened ones, for higher power, power that you could only dream of in your pathetic

161

life as a fucking editor of a fucking newspaper. Me marry a fucking editor, what a joke. And it didn't take long to get you into bed, did it, work your charm I was told, and you weren't even a good lay, then leave him to us, because once we had the goods on you getting a little underage pussy and snuffing out one of the little bastards, your Daddy would be putty in our hands. Couldn't bring shame on the family name, so all those secrets he holds so close to his chest would be ours to use. All along you were too fucking, goddam stupid to realise that we only ever wanted your Daddy, and I should have known that mousy little pommie bitch wouldn't be too far behind you, what are you fucking her now? I always knew she was gagging for it."

I moved to Christian's side to comfort him, he had just stood there, speechless, letting Candace rant her vile tirade. Sadly, Candace had more to say.

"That's it Julia, go join my spineless cunt of a husband." Before she could hurl further insults King thankfully intervened, "I think we've all heard enough ma'am" before he forced the gag back into her mouth, she didn't stop even with it in place, luckily it was now inaudible.

As King gave the order for his men to take the captives away, I had to make sure Christian was alright, he still hadn't said a word, his eyes firmly planted on the figure of Candace, who was now being hauled up and made ready for transport.

"Say something Christian please, you're scaring me" I pleaded.

"What is there to say Julia, I've been played for a fool." Knowing my friend well I decided to let him take his time in expressing his feelings, we would talk later, heart to heart as old friends do.

As the captives were lined up, I perused the group, apart from Candace, her parents and airport man, there were three others, all men, I thought it strange that Ramirez wasn't amongst them. I didn't have the foggiest idea who they were, and made a mental note to myself to find out later. For now Christian was my main concern, also we had the revelations to face that Payne had warned us to prepare ourselves for.

I was confused, the captives weren't being led back along the corridor to the staircase, but further into the underground tunnel. "I thought they were being taken back to the ship," I said aloud.

The answer to my question came from one of King's men, "Ma'am this tunnel leads straight to the edge of the island, there's an entrance door, carefully camouflaged, not far from the dock area."

"Oh my God, that's how they transferred the children from the boats without detection, no doubt under the cover of darkness too. They had every base covered". I replied.

Joining the conversation, King added, "Yes, that sums their operation up well, they won't be so high and mighty once they are charged in a court of law with crimes against humanity, which believe me that's where they're heading, and just to let you know they won't be travelling back with us, that would only complicate matters further, they are being taken straight to mainland USA, a plane is already on its way."

"Well let's pray the court is in a State that still carries the death penalty, as I for one want to see them hang, long drop, short rope suits me fine." I couldn't believe I'd just said those words, I'd always been vehemently against any form of capital punishment, not now, let the bastards swing.

Regret at my words voiced out loud surged through me, how would Christian feel if his wife did indeed swing from a rope. "Christian, forgive me, I shouldn't have said that, but it's how I feel."

His reply was instant, without anger but tinged with sadness. "That wasn't the woman I thought I married, may God have mercy on her black soul."

Clearing his throat to garner our attention, King motioned us forward towards the corridor. Taking the lead, talking as he made his way to the first door on his left, he swung it wide open...

"We need to be heading back to the ship pretty soon, so have a look around, it'll give you an idea of what this has been used for. I'm going to leave a couple of my guys down here with you, the rest of us are going to scout around upstairs for anymore incriminating evidence, electronic devices etc that may hold leads further up the chain. You have thirty minutes."

With that he turned on his heel and left us to explore and to discover for ourselves what secrets this subterranean space held.

The mood amongst us was sombre, dark and almost hesitant, as if to finally witness first hand the lair of these monsters would confirm our worst and deepest fears, of a wicked and despicable underworld, where monsters preyed on the most innocent.

Inhaling deeply, I addressed Christian, David, Raul and Daniel, "My heart is telling me I don't want to do this, but my head is telling me I need to see it all with my own eyes, are we all ready?" They all nodded agreement in unison.

There were fourteen dungeon-like rooms, seven on each side of the corridor. Ten contained two single camp like beds, a small table between and a toilet. Apart from the smell of damp, everything was clean, you could almost describe it as immaculate, obviously ready and prepared for the arrival of the children.

One much larger room held a large communal showering area, with four large showerheads descending from the ceiling, four wash basins too. It resembled a summer camp where the facilities were utilitarian, basic but adequate. Seemingly innocuous, if you weren't already aware of who would be using them.

As we moved from room to room, nobody spoke, each of us locked in our own world of thought and reflection, that was until we reached the room that contained a kitchen.

Again, innocuous enough at first sight. Only as I noticed boxes and boxes of mac and cheese on the counter, the comfort food that children the world over adored, the same variety my own children always asked for on our many family holidays to the US, I broke my silence, my voice breaking, "Comfort food, my God, the irony of it."

Unable to speak further for fear of physically breaking down, I made to leave the room as Raul opened the door to an enormous refrigerator, he delved inside it and held out in his hand a tub of Gel O, shaking his head as he spoke. "Good Lord above, these sick bastards were lulling the poor children into a sense of security, feeding them what all kids love before they used them for God knows what."

Unable to acknowledge Raul's statement verbally, I managed a nod and exited the kitchen. However, the tenuous hold over my composure was completely lost at what confronted me in the next room. Taking several seconds to register, almost as if my brain was fighting to acknowledge what its contents signified.

Fully kitted out, it was for all intents and purposes a doctor's surgery, complete with an examination table, what looked very much like a dentists' chair, and large overhead lights synonymous with operating theatres.

That was enough for me, I had no need to see more of its contents. Claustrophobia was engulfing my entire being, a cloak of darkness wrapping itself around me, making breathing almost impossible, yet rendering me unable to stop my brain from conjuring up images as to what on earth was the purpose for this room.

"I've seen enough, I need to get out of here and breathe fresh air before I vomit."

Not waiting for any responses nor needing any, I made my way along the tunnel to the staircase, stopping briefly to regain my composure before beginning the climb. I didn't stop until I'd reached the wraparound veranda, even ignoring one of King's men when he tried to stand in my way and firmly ask me, "Ma'am where do you think you're going? Our orders are to keep you all together."

Sidestepping him, I replied, "I need air, so please tell your Boss I'll wait outside for the others to join me."

Once outside I filled my lungs with deep cleansing gasps of fresh air, before sitting down on the top step. To gather myself together and attempt to portray outwardly at least my ability to handle the scenes from what I now most definitely viewed as the dungeon.

Completely lost in thought, totally unaware that the Guys had re-joined me until Christian plonked himself down on the step by my side. "You OK babe?" he enquired.

"Yep," I replied. Fearing further conversation would unleash the tears I was struggling to contain, I simply laid my head on his shoulder, his nearness was enough to comfort me.

A flurry of activity ensued, following the barking of orders by King. Payne and several of his men could then be seen carrying large black sacks to one of the golf carts, the contents of which I presumed contained the incriminating evidence they'd sought.

Before making our way to the transport, something so moving it left me humbled took place. Raul, David and Daniel took turns to hug me, real bear hugs, a show of solidarity I did not expect from two hardened police officers and an ex-spook.

With little time for words, David acted as spokesman for them all and earnestly spoke aloud.

"We know that was gut wrenching, even for us, but remember without you and your strength and determination, we would not be here, and those sick bastards would be free, you are one hell of a lady Julia."

The tears I had succeeded in keeping at bay were now helplessly cascading down my face, an unstoppable torrent of emotion had been unleashed and I was incapable of stopping it. I was physically and emotionally exhausted, drained, however an inner voice was rearing its head amidst all the tumult swirling around my brain that there were more revelations to come, much would be made clearer.

The cryptic and subconscious message pulled me up short, and served to stem my tears. My spirits bolstered somewhat, I managed a weak smile of thanks, not trusting my voice, and walked silently to the golf carts.

All I yearned for now was to get as far away as possible from this island that held untold horrors, and the innate feeling of darkness threatening to cover me in a cloak of despair at the depths of cruelty some humans would and could inflict on fellow members of the human race.

Chapter 25

Warm Caribbean air infused with the salt from waves created by our boats path served as a balm to soothe us on our journey back to the cutter.

Fortunately the earlier storm had dissipated, disappearing as quickly as it had arrived. Eerily giving credence to my wayward thought it had been sent as a supernatural warning of unfolding secrets soon to be revealed on the Island of St. Lucy.

A heaven sent message of God's anger? Crazy thought I acknowledged to myself, but then if I imagined my life as little as a month ago, would I ever have believed I'd be here now, no I'd think I was indeed crazy.

A hive of activity greeted us when we were finally back on board the ship and she was made ready to set a course for the return trip to Haiti.

Once the anchor was hoisted and we were on our way, Captain Pendleton gestured for us to join him.

"Before you get cleaned up and grab some rest, I've been instructed to get you up to speed with the situation at hand, so you are fully prepared and aware of what is waiting for you all back in Haiti."

Crikey this sounded ominous, and a multitude of scenarios flashed through my mind, all of which were so far from the correct one, I was miles out. Turning my concentration back to Captain Pendleton I listened with growing astonishment.

"The Embassy have tried to keep a lid on events, however it appears someone, at present unidentified, has leaked certain details of what went down at the coffee plantation, to be totally blunt with you all, the shit has hit the proverbial fan."

He went on to add;

"As we speak William Monroe and his staff are working their butts off, to contain all the heat coming your way and are trying to second guess the Haitian Government's reaction. It can go one of two ways. The first is they'll accuse you of carrying out a covert and unsanctioned act on foreign soil or second, be damned grateful those kids were rescued and try to spin it, that they were fully aware and sanctioned it and share in what will no doubt be public praise. Let's all hope and pray it's the latter."

After several minutes of stunned silence, and only when Captain Pendleton's words had been fully digested by us all, did the questions start to be asked and David was first out of the blocks.

"How the hell did anything get leaked, we were assured everything was watertight, all dealt with in house, something goddam well stinks here, that's a certain."

Daniel and Raul were talking quietly between themselves, then Daniel spoke "Either of the two scenarios puts Raul and me in possible jeopardy, my friends' you are more than aware of the corruption in my country and human trafficking makes big money and with that greedy politicians and government officials have their silence handsomely paid for. But the cycle has to be broken, how else can we end the terrible trade if we do not find the courage to stand up for what we have all willingly taken our part in. Did the island not make you all more determined to play a part, however small to help eradicate such evil?"

Captain Pendleton was the first to reply, "Sir, it is not often I find myself humbled in this fucked up world of ours, I sure as hell am now, you are a very brave and honourable man, it's a damned shame there aren't more like you."

A spontaneous round of applause followed and Daniel looked emotional. The last few days had affected us all, male, female, gender played no part in raw emotion and empathy, just the pure belief that we could all play our part in aiding fellow members of the human race. A strong conviction that good will prevail over evil was all that was required.

As we had absolutely no clue whatsoever as to the identity of the leaker, add to that fact we were stuck on a boat in the middle of the Caribbean Sea, with a long journey before us, we unanimously decided there wasn't a great deal to be achieved until we reached the Embassy.

We were however united in the belief that William, would be at this very moment, moving heaven and earth to locate the leaker and using everything at his disposal to protect us. Damage limitation expertise was surely a prerequisite of being a diplomat!

With all that in mind, all I wanted at this particular moment in time, was a long, hot shower and a change of clothes. To cleanse my body of any trace I still had from the island. To rid myself of the smell of damp that had permeated the underground lair and the smell of blood and brain matter still present under my nose.

I grabbed my rucksack from the bunk and made my way to the bathroom facilities, being the only woman on board had its plus points, I got to shower first and on my own.

I luxuriated in the steaming hot water, standing under the showerhead for what felt like an eternity, until any trace of the island had been well and truly washed away. It was a cathartic experience, my body and indeed my mind purged for the time being at least.

Knowing that although I was exhausted, sleep would not be forthcoming, I made my way on deck. Dawn was breaking, so whilst the guys showered I took the opportunity of a few minutes on my own. I marvelled at the glorious colours exploding before my eyes, as the first rays of sunlight shimmered across the Caribbean Sea, Mother Nature at her finest.

Lost in deep thought I didn't hear the approaching footsteps, only when Christian coughed to announce his presence did I realise he was standing beside me.

"Hey, I'm sorry to intrude, you looked so peaceful, but Julia we need to talk and now might be the only time we get this place to ourselves."

He looked so serious, I was a little perturbed, nervous even, at what he wanted to discuss. I have never felt uncomfortable with Christian, but a frisson of anxiety pulsed through me. Not wanting him to see my concern, I plastered a big smile on my face and replied.

"Where shall we start my darling? So much has happened I couldn't possibly know where to start."

"There's a great deal I need to get off my chest right now, if I don't do it, I might never get the chance, carpe diem and all that."

Turning from the rail I'd been leaning on to face him, I reached out to gently touch his hand before I spoke. "It's been a torrid time for all of us, especially you, Christian, so I'm here and ready to listen, there really is nothing we can't talk openly about."

Looking up at the sky, inhaling deeply as he prepared to unburden himself, he then gazed intently down at me and the outpouring began.

"I have pretty much had my private life served up on a platter for you all to witness, as soul destroying and degrading as that was, the worst part of all involved Candace maligning you. I could just about bear her admitting she'd married me as an ulterior motive, although never in a million years would I have thought it was anything other than for Dad's political connections, not as a ruse to blackmail him over honey trapping me in their sick activities. I knew she harboured deep feelings of resentment and jealousy concerning our friendship, she could never understand there wasn't a sexual element to it. I know you've never seen me as anything other than a dear and cherished friend."

Oh God I had to interrupt him by placing my fingers on his lips, I knew in my heart of hearts where this leading and suddenly felt terribly afraid to hear anymore.

Christian swiped my fingers away and carried on. "No, you have to hear this Julia, I've always loved you, but I knew I could never have you in the way I wanted. From the start it was always you and Steve, childhood sweethearts, so I settled for second best. My dad knew, in a way only a parent can, I

170

told him it was enough just to have you in my life, but after all the shit of the last few days, it served as a wake up call. When that guy attacked you at the plantation, I'd never known panic and sheer terror like it, yet you were so cool with it, I've never known a woman like you Julia and I never will. I love every bit of you and I want every bit of you too."

Christian's outburst had rendered me speechless, unable to articulate a response, he took my silence as reciprocation and placing his hands around my face, and with an expression of pure adulation writ large upon his handsome face, leant down to kiss me.

In any other universe perhaps, I would have welcomed this open display of forbidden love, however with emotions running high on all levels and guilt coursing through my veins I resisted.

"Christian, please not now, if you profess to love me as deeply as you have proclaimed, give me time to process it, I'm feeling pretty vulnerable right now and I have a husband and children to consider."

My reply served to cool Christian's ardour somewhat, "I've been honest with you, you need to be honest with yourself now, I've laid my soul bare, put my cards on the table."

Gathering myself together from the shock of Christian's revelation, all I could manage was a feeble response "Let's get the next few days over with and before I fly back to the UK, I promise you we will sort this out."

But Christian wasn't finished "Be honest with me I beg you, have you ever had feelings other than platonic towards me?"

The pure unadulterated and raw passion in his voice called to me on such a profound level. Stirring me in a way I hadn't realised still existed in my middle-aged body, it could only warrant unfettered candour in response.

"Yes!"

With the tumult of emotions over the last few days, I could now add betrayal to the ever expanding list. My head started to throb with the intensity of it all, oh Christian your timing was just bloody awful.

I left Christian on deck and he had the good grace not to follow. I sought my bunk, at least I'd try to feign sleep. Reaching it, I laid on my side, facing inwards, desperate for sleep to come but knowing with my mind so full, it would evade me.

Miraculously I did eventually fall into a deep, blissfully unencumbered and uninterrupted sleep. By my estimation I'd slept for seven hours, that left another seven before we arrived back in Haiti.

Grabbing my notepad from my rucksack, I decided to put pen to paper and begin to write down my account of this incredible journey, it would also serve as a ruse for me to be left alone by the others. Praise be it worked.

Writing had always been my passion and I dived into it with relish, wanting my recollections to be recorded whilst still fresh and vivid in my mind. Determined it would take all my concentration, allowing no time to reflect on the situation with Christian and I.

Raul thoughtfully brought me food and drink, his only comment being "once a journalist always a journalist my friend." His sweet and jovial demeanour served to raise my spirits, smiling back at him I replied, "Oh yes Raul, the first rule of journalism is always to write it down, thank you for the food too."

Fortunately, he must have sensed my need for solitude as he quickly left without further comment, just a playful wink of an eye.

I'd always preferred to write in longhand, it gave me more of a connection to my writing, only committing it to a computer once I was happy with it. Even though I'd been busy scribbling for hours, it was nowhere near finished when I heard voices approaching.

Hearing Christian's voice gave me a flutter in my belly "Julia, we have to pack our stuff up now, we're forty minutes away from Haiti and King wants to update us."

Not wanting to make eye contact, I grabbed my rucksack, stuffed my notepad into it and rose from the bunk.

Trying to make light of an awkward situation I retorted "Ready for duty Sir," and saluted him before making my way to the command room.

King wasted no time on commencing his update, we had barely sat down before he began.

"OK Guys, there's no way to sugar coat this, the shit has indeed hit the fan. So, the plan is to head it off from the start, to meet fire with fire. Official channels have all been fully debriefed and they've directed that there be a press conference called. As you are all fully and painfully aware, I might add, that the desire to eradicate human trafficking is gaining momentum and there is huge public support worldwide for action, so that's the angle we are going to take, emphasizing on the humanitarian role you guys have played. That said we are also aware of the widespread corruption trafficking generates and it has become abundantly clear that even our embassies' and their staff are not immune to it. Ergo I insist when you reach the embassy you under no circumstance discuss any details whatsoever with any member of the embassy staff, and that is to also include the Ambassador, before the press conference. The situation will be made clearer to you, once we have dealt with the press."

The last part of King's speech raised a few eyebrows amongst us, but when pressed on it by Christian, King shut him down instantly, firmly and in no uncertain terms replied that the subject was not up for further discussion.

My naturally inquisitive nature was now in overdrive mode. Finally coming to the conclusion the leaker must have been identified, why wait until after the press conference though?

The remainder of the time we had left on the boat was spent with King and Payne coaching us on what we should and shouldn't reveal to the press pack, who they were in no doubt would be wanting a warts and all account now they had the scent of a juicy story. They were without a moral compass, just desperate to keep their ratings up.

Under no circumstance were we to mention the island or anything relating to King and his team. It was imperative their identities remain totally secret for obvious reasons. The only topic up for discussion was the rescue of the orphans at the coffee plantation. If questions were asked about fatalities, the reply was to be "no comment", ditto if we felt unsure regarding any question they might pose.

King went on to add William Monroe would lead the press conference, alongside him would be a representative of the Haitian Government and a high ranking Police official. Was I naive in thinking this was positive news, interpreting their presence as confirmation a tide was indeed turning in Haiti? I'd pray hard for it to be so.

Chapter 26

After expressing our thanks and gratitude to Captain Pendleton and his crew it was time to disembark the boat and make our way to the Embassy. If my world had seemed almost surreal during the last few days, it was beginning to feel inordinately so now, as I tried to prepare myself for the press conference and all the consequences being thrust into the media spotlight would undoubtedly bring.

Hence the instruction from King to make contact with our loved ones at home. He said it was imperative we warn them in advance of the press conference. It might not be carried by major international news outlets, but social media with its worldwide audience, was a totally different matter. It could possibly be shared to millions of people on every continent on the planet within hours, a sobering thought.

It was late in the evening when we finally drove through the gates of the US Embassy in Port au Prince. The blacked out windows of the SUV's afforded us privacy until we reached the back of the building, it seemed our identities would only be revealed once the cameras started to roll.

An air of urgency permeated the building, it was palpable. A member of staff wasted no time in directing us to side rooms, handing us in turn mobile phones, informing us we had ten minutes, then shutting the door on their way out.

A mixture of trepidation and relief surged through me as I dialled Steve's mobile phone number. Relief at finally being able to speak to my husband, swiftly followed by an intense dose of trepidation. How would he handle the news of his wife's imminent exposure to the awaiting press pack? I pressed the green button before I lost my nerve.

Answering on the third ring Steve's voice came through loud and clear, as if he were in the room next door, not thousands of miles away. I dived straight in with the speech I'd rehearsed in my head during the journey back from the boat.

"Steve, it's me Julia, I don't have long so please just listen until I've finished explaining everything. We were successful in saving twelve beautiful children from a disused coffee plantation, it served as a holding place before they would have been transported elsewhere. The traffickers were all eliminated, bar one, he was taken alive and brought back to the Embassy for interrogation and he sung like a canary. Giving up all sorts of information on the cartel he works for, I will explain more on this when I get home. Now for the main reason of my phone call, there's been a leak from someone inside the Embassy and the press have gotten hold of it. So, to head off any potential backlash it's been decided to meet it head on and hold a press conference, which will be going live shortly. I'll be in it along with Christian and the most incredible and brave men who volunteered to join us and help save the children." I finally came up for air and awaited Steve's response. I purposely hadn't included any mention of the trip to the island and all the horrors that entailed, that could definitely wait until I arrived home.

"All I want to know is, are you safe? I've been going bloody crazy here with precious little contact from you. I'm glad you saved the kids don't get me wrong, but I want you home before you're involved in anymore hare-brained escapades that I've got to explain to our own kids."

Well that reply brought me up short, and I hesitated to find the right words in response. "Please don't be angry, I'm safe and being well taken care of, I'll be home in a few days and we'll gather the kids together and I will explain everything then. Please for now call and warn them of the press conference, chances are it won't receive much attention in the UK anyway, but social media is a concern, and Steve it's been much, much more than a hare-brained escapade, that has hurt me deeply. Tell the kids I love them and I really must hang up now."

Not wishing to wait for another reprimand from my husband I did indeed hang up, spending the rest of my ten minutes reflecting on why I was unable to tell Steve I loved him. Perhaps Christian's declaration had affected me more than I was willing to admit to. Pushing those thoughts away I left the room and handed the mobile phone back to the member of staff waiting outside.

Determined not to give any hint of the disappointment my phone call had resulted in, I casually strolled to re-join the others. Making damn sure I had a smile on my face, in absolute contradiction to the anger slowly rising in me at my husband's flippant description of what had been a truly momentous few days, the personal impact of which I was certain would stay with me for the rest of my life.

The time was nearing to face the next hurdle. As a journalist I'd attended many press conferences, albeit in the audience, there to report on it, now the roles would be reversed, I wouldn't be asking the questions but answering them. Karma can be a bitch, ready to bite when least expected.

Thank God I had a few minutes to tidy myself up and grab a coffee. A few minutes had passed when I heard William's voice, having my back to his approaching figure I turned to greet him.

Shock tore through me, gone was the suave and sophisticated diplomat I'd previously met. To be replaced by a man seemingly with the weight of the world on his broad shoulders. His eyes were red rimmed, that look you get when sleep is not forthcoming, his once immaculate hair untidy and his suit appeared crumpled, even his tie was slightly askew.

Flanking him on either side were two men in uniform who I surmised were the Haitian officials. Behind them more men in uniforms, this time however they wore the insignia of a United States Embassy.

My immediate analysis of the situation was the shit had well and truly hit the proverbial fan, and from the shocked facial expressions of Raul, David, Christian and Daniel it appeared they'd formed the same opinion.

Pangs of guilt wracked me, what had we exposed William to? But hadn't he remarked previously his ambivalence of any repercussions he might face; confusion was writ large on my face.

He didn't give us long to ponder further, announcing abruptly and with little decorum. "Let's get this over with".

William and the entourage headed straight for the conference room door, and we followed in meek, almost subjugated silence.

Entering the room, I sneaked a look to my left, needing to ascertain how big the press pack in attendance would be. The room was almost full, given the late hour and little notification time, it left me surprised to say the least.

Quickly turning my attention back to the seating arrangements on the long table at the front of the room, I noticed only three nameplates in the middle. William was one, with presumably the two Haitian officials placed either side of his. Good at least our names weren't there for all to see and identify.

Taking a seat between Christian and Raul, I waited for the conference to start. As William commenced his opening lines the familiar sound of camera shutters began, almost drowning out his voice. He gave the photographers short shrift.

"Ladies and Gentlemen, you will have ample opportunity to take your photographs, why don't we first concentrate on the reason for you all being here, without the incessant noise of your cameras."

Thank goodness it did the trick, allowing us to concentrate on the questions being asked. Within twenty minutes we were done and dusted. Steered by William and the two Haitian officials, we gave the barest of details, enough to satisfy their need to fill headlines, without divulging too much information.

It was a whole lot easier than I'd initially feared, largely owing to William's insistence that at a later date further details would be released, he seemed as eager as the rest of us to bring it to a swift closure. For that I owed him a huge debt of gratitude.

However, William's whole demeanour gave me cause for concern, although the room's air conditioning kept all present cool, he appeared to be sweating profusely, constantly using a handkerchief to mop his brow. His hands were also visibly shaking, leaving me nonplussed as to why.

The Embassy's security staff curiously instructed all those at the top table to remain seated, apart from the two Haitian government officials. Whilst others escorted them and the press pack from the room via double doors at the back. Once they were vacated, things started to take a bizarre and worrying turn, as the security staff positioned themselves in front of both sets of doors, effectively blocking off any exit.

As a myriad of reasons for this swirled around in my brain, William rose from his seat, and made his way to the doors, only for his path to be blocked. He launched a tirade of abuse "Get out of my fucking way you pricks, I am still the Ambassador and I order you to stand the fuck down."

Before an answer was forthcoming from the security guards, the doors were opened and I sat in stunned silence at what began to unfold, never in a million years would I have guessed correctly the scenario about to be played out before my very own eyes.

Two security guards approached William from behind, as one of the men who had entered the room began to recite William's rights and place him under arrest. William fought furiously against handcuffs being used to restrain him. It was horrifying to witness, what the fuck had just happened, were they coming for us next?

We didn't have long to wait for an explanation. After William was literally dragged, unceremoniously from the room, King and Payne appeared and gathered in front of us alongside several grey suited, very serious looking men.

What followed was a full and frank disclosure, leaving Raul, Christian, David, Daniel and I reeling with shock and in utter disbelief. We were rendered speechless.

It transpired William was in fact responsible for the leaking of information, arrogantly believing he'd covered his tracks sufficiently enough for it not to be traced back to him. This being only a part of his web of deception.

Listening with mounting incredulity everything was laid bare, all the pieces of the puzzle woven together culminating into a crescendo of revelations so breathtaking they caused a revolting ball of nausea to form in my belly.

It appeared William had been under suspicion for some time and was being closely watched. A consummate actor, he'd lulled us all into a false sense of security and trust. His communications unbeknown to him were all intercepted, and information gathered to build a picture of his involvement in nefarious activities.

Again, we were told how fortuitous the timing of our arrival had been, giving good cover for the need to involve the elite forces of King and his teams. They had carried out a dual mission, assisting us and at the same time searching for further evidence against William. The island had provided a treasure trove of information.

Believing all evidence of his many trips to St. Lucy had been destroyed he hadn't counted on his lover Candace keeping photographs and videos of his participation in their sordid activities. Hence King's announcement of a search for laptops etc, when we were on the island. It had reaped dividends, as did the safe, which held further incriminating evidence.

The Clays it appeared were not averse to using blackmail on their daughter's lover. William's double life had enabled them to be untouchable, always several steps ahead of the law.

William had been willing to even sacrifice his old friend Christian. It was horrible enough to carry out an illicit affair with his friends' wife, he took it to a much higher and sinister level.

By intercepting his messages of warning, changing them and the replies sent in return from Candace, the Clays were in complete ignorance of our impending visit to their luxurious island. Hence the total shock and surprise of our arrival and the preceding one of King and his men.

By leaking details of the rescue at the coffee plantation, King surmised William's plan was to direct the heat and subsequent attention towards us and away from the island. Fortunately he'd completely underestimated the desire for change slowly taking place within the Haitian Government, prompted by the efforts of a new US administration and worldwide growing awareness and condemnation of human trafficking.

In summing up William had been fucked in every way possible, and had been completely oblivious to the incredible operation put in place to take him down.

Being so immensely engrossed in King's dialogue I hadn't thought that yet again Christian was openly subjected to colossal humiliation. To find out in such fashion that your wife, albeit estranged was knocking off someone he'd considered an old and loyal friend would be devastating. Without regard to what had taken place between us only a few hours earlier, I did what I would always have done before his declaration, I hugged him so hard and uttered soothing words of comfort, that only he could hear.

King graciously offered some words of apology, but insisted there was no other way to handle the situation. That William had been confronted with the overwhelming evidence against him and told in no uncertain terms to play his part in return for a closed-door trial, or the alternative, to face public humiliation.

Christian was magnanimous in accepting King's explanation, took it like the gentleman he has always been, but it must have felt like yet another knife in his gut, the pain excruciating and seemingly without end.

With little more to add and fortunately the cognitive ability to understand our need for privacy after such far reaching and devastating revelations King brought the discussion to a close. Adding a final few words.

"You all need to get some rest, be back here at 09.00 hours tomorrow morning for the final debrief. By then we should have travel arrangements etc in place to get Julia, David and Christian out of here."

He turned and left the room. For several minutes we sat in silence, an awkward limbo spawning between us. We had been through so much together, been so strong and supportive of each other, I refused to allow our final few hours in each other's company be reduced to this. I didn't hold back.

"Come on Guys, we've been through so much in such a short time, given each other the strength to carry on when all seemed lost and hopeless. I'm so humbled to call all of you my friend, and I will thank God each and every day for the gift of your friendship and support, we mustn't part ways not feeling able to talk to each other."

Thankfully it did the trick, the chasm closed with warm words that filled the empty space between us. The momentary despair that threatened to fill my heart replaced with renewed optimism; our tightly knit group was back on track. Who knew what the future held, perhaps one day we would reunite for another crusade.

A knock on the door robbed us of extra time to convey our thoughts and begrudgingly we parted company, only after bear hugs all round.

I was shown back to the room I'd previously stayed in. As I glanced around it, I took a moment to reflect on the seismic events I had been witness to since I last slept here. They seemed too incredible, too farfetched, yet all too real.

In all honesty I felt far too overwrought to analyse events further, and eyeing the robe so thoughtfully laid out on the bed made me yearn for a long hot bath before I succumbed to its enveloping softness.

As I lay on the bed, the effects of the warm bath water leaving me relaxed for the first time in days, wrapped up in the soft robe, a light tap on the door broke my reverie. I rose from the bed almost resentful at the intrusion, wondering what on earth could be so important it warranted disturbance at this late hour.

Tentatively opening the door my eyes fell on Christian, standing there in front of me. Not giving me a chance to question why, he crossed the threshold into my room, kicking the door closed behind him, urgency radiating from him, hot and intense, invisible yet palpable. We stood facing each other, our eyes locked, for what felt like an eternity, both lost to the desire mounting between us.

Christian broke the interminable silence. "Give me one night, let me taste what could have been."

That one sentence lit the fuse paper of lust, filling me with a passion I no longer thought myself capable of. The years tumbling away like rockfall from a mountain, rendering me giddy with wanton abandonment.

He poured every single ounce of love and longing into that first kiss and I freely, unreservedly without inhibition matched his growing ardour, inch by delicious inch.

Forcing images of my husband far from my mind, knowing I'd face my guilt later, I accepted Christian's hand as he led me to the bed. I knew I wanted him as desperately as he wanted me.

Our love making was gentle, unhurried and sublime, as we took pleasure in pleasing each other, both reaching our climax together. That pinnacle of oneness leaving us sated, but wanting more.

We were wrapped in each other's arms, and as corny as it sounds, basking in the afterglow of our lovemaking. That wonderful feeling only reached when you have been united as one, the ultimate act of intimacy between two people, ours especially as the fruit had been forbidden for so long.

My only words as I took his beautiful face in my hands were, "Let's not talk, it can all wait till the morning, I just want to hold onto this for as long as I can."

He showed his tacit agreement by tenderly kissing me and then whispered, "I don't want to sleep to waste a moment of this night together."

We lay awake for a while before sleep claimed us, still wrapped around each other like a vine, not willing or able to let go for a second.

Chapter 27

The Revelation

Sleep led me to a well trodden path, one I was all too familiar with, where my subconscious state tuned into the voices of children. My gift to act as a conduit or earth Mother, the gift that had led me halfway across the world, was coming to me with force in the twilight hours.

The channel was clear and their determination to converse with me stronger than at any time I'd previously experienced. Yet these voices were in English and not the Haitian Creole of recent visits, making it so much easier for me to grasp and instantly understand.

These pure and beautiful souls were not pleading for help this time, their ethereal presence was being used to offer explanation of times and events from many years ago. From the deep recesses of my memory, flashbacks began appearing to me alongside the voices.

I felt as though I was being sucked into a vortex, spiralling down to another dimension, one in which I appeared young again. Accompanying the flashbacks were voices like a soundtrack to a movie.

The first featured me standing by a car on what I could only describe as the hard shoulder of a busy road, staring down in dismay at a puncture in one of the tyres.

I instantly recalled the evening of Friday the 6th of March 1987, a night in a lifetime of lifetimes I would never be able to forget.

Excitedly making my way to the ferry port of Zeebrugge to catch a ferry to England. My first trip home since I'd started work on the Belgium desk of the newspaper I'd been working for.

My trusted little Ford Fiesta was going nowhere, oh how I'd regretted at the time not listening to Steve and my Dad when they'd futilely tried to encourage me to learn to change a tyre. It was several hours before a kindly man stopped to help me, by this time I'd missed my sailing, however I was sure there were further sailings that night and made my way to the port.

The port a scene of pandemonium when I eventually arrived. Amid all the panic I managed to learn of the terrible disaster that had befallen the ferry Herald of Free Enterprise, the very same one due to take me home.

A punctured tyre had saved my life!.

Then came the second flashback, I was reliving the two most phenomenal events of my life in quick succession.

Fast forward to the 21st December 1988, and my dream job of covering the US desk of the newspaper. Due to start on the 2nd of January, Steve and I would take the opportunity of spending Christmas together in New York before I began my six month secondment. Our flights and hotel were booked, the excitement almost unbearable.

Then the pain in my side started, becoming so intense that an ambulance was called, and in the early hours of the 21st of December 1988, after being rushed into theatre for an emergency operation, my appendix was successfully removed.

An appendectomy had prevented me from boarding Pan Am flight 103! bound for New York via Heathrow.

So many images swirling around my head, a snowstorm of memories bombarding me as I viewed them, a bystander bearing witness to past events of my own life.

The voices became louder and in unison, "Mother you were saved for this time, your gift of sight so strong, your love for humanity powerful, your belief in God unshaken. You were chosen to save the children."

I was being pulled from the vortex, I fought the hands seeking to bring me back to the here and now, "No" I screamed frantically, I couldn't leave that place yet. I was desperate to know more.

As if a curtain had been closed, my mind went blank, a screen of black descended and my body felt as though it were rising to the surface of a deep dark sea, after having plunged to its murky depths.

I channelled my attention to a man's voice, urgent in its tone. "Come back to me baby, please come back to me."

Confusion wracked me as I fought my way back to the present, the voice acting as a guide to steer my path through the confines of the pitch black darkness surrounding me.

Gradually the room came into focus, my eyes adjusting to the light and I recognised Christian's beautiful, though agonised face peering down at me.

Fighting a deluge of tears, I tried to form words coherent enough for him to understand. After several attempts I managed to say, "They came back to show me Christian."

"I know baby, I woke up as you were talking in your sleep, you became so distressed I had to try and wake you up, to bring you back."

Cocooned in his arms, my equilibrium regained, he lay patiently as I began to elucidate details of the visit, not interrupting only listening. Allowing me to share the phenomenal revelations from the spirit realm.

Only after I'd finished the astonishing and earth shattering disclosures did Christian speak.

The timbre of his voice low and soothing Christian responded. "I remember all of it, we'd spoken on the telephone the day you were due to catch the ferry home, when news of the disaster came through the wires I was frantic with worry, the hours before I found out you were alive and safe felt like days. As for the Christmas of '88, thank God your Mom telephoned to tell me you were sick and not to go to the airport and meet your flight, I honestly don't how I would've coped had she not done that. Thinking I'd lost you from my life all over again, you see I was in love with you even then".

His voice broke on that last sentence, but he carried on "The countless times I plucked up the courage to tell you, only to lose my nerve at the last minute."

I honestly never realised he'd had these feelings for me, still reeling from seeing such profound parts of my life in action replay left me unable to articulate a response, my concentration on much more recent matters.

The guilt I'd carried for years regarding why I had escaped two tragedies and not all those other poor souls lifting slowly from my shoulders, assuaged somewhat now by knowing I'd been saved for some future plan other worldly forces had mapped out for me.

"Christian please not now, I'm struggling enough to comprehend how my life has been preordained without having you make me go on a mammoth guilt trip for not realising you've been in love with me all these years and not forgetting I've committed the cardinal sin of adultery too."

The wake up call worked, snapping Christian from his self-indulgent reflections to the here and now.

"Julia I'm sorry, that was so selfish of me, I got carried away in the moment, not knowing when I'd have the chance again to be so candid, I've told you I want you, you need to make a choice."

"I know and I will, first I need to return home and see my children, explain everything about the trip face to face, I owe them that at least. And for now all I want is to lay here quietly in your arms and savour this time we have together."

After kissing me tenderly Christian replied, "I can live with that."

I awoke to the sound of my mobile phone alarm, I'd set it for 8 a.m. giving me an hour before the debrief with King.

Christian was still sleeping soundly, I recalled the joke at university of his legendary ability to sleep through literally anything, he hadn't changed.

I took the opportunity to drink in every detail of his beautiful face. His hair was greying, the inevitable lines of age had formed around his eyes and forehead, but he was still a striking man. Butterflies were performing arabesques in my belly, their fluttering wings leaving me flushed and with a deep inner warmth.

"Christian, wake up, you should go back to your room, before anyone sees you."

Dressing quickly he slipped out of my room, blowing kisses as he went. Oh God, how could I love two men at once? Not wanting to dwell on the matter any further I leapt out of bed and headed for the bathroom.

Chapter 28

2 Timothy 4:7
I have fought the good fight,
I have finished the course,
I have kept the faith.

Walking into the conference room I found all the guys helping themselves to a buffet style breakfast that had thoughtfully been laid out for us. Having no appetite, I helped myself to a large mug of steaming black coffee and took a seat at the table.

King introduced the two members of consular staff accompanying him and Payne. One thought crossed my mind, for a civilian King appeared to be on a level footing with the diplomatic staff and indeed with the official secret service officers who had been present at William's arrest. Not being terribly au fait with the machinations of diplomatic protocol I still found it strange.

Daniel and Raul were told they were to report back for duty immediately following the end of this meeting, they seemed genuinely pleased and relieved to still have their jobs.

Then attention was directed at David, apparently, he'd already informed King of his intention to cross back over into the Dominican Republic, as he had other leads to follow up on. But needed to keep his head down and lie low for a few months, let the dust settle from the press conference.

That left Christian and I. With our identities out there for all the world to see, the need for us to covertly slip back across the border and travel home via the Dominican Republic was now deemed null and void.

Christian had been booked on an early afternoon American Airlines flight out of Port Au Prince bound for Washington DC via Miami.

My flight home to Heathrow would also take me via Miami, with a five hour layover I had a long trip ahead of me.

I was thankful for this time alone, time that would be spent in deep contemplation of everything that had transpired over the recent weeks.

My life had changed irrevocably in many ways, some welcome some not. I would not be the same woman boarding the flight to Miami, compared to the woman who had boarded the flight in London, that much was crystal clear.

As our flights were only an hour apart Christian and I would be driven to the airport together. I prayed he wouldn't use this time to press me for a decision.

All this had been organised in just a few hours. Impressive indeed, and I offered my sincere thanks to all those involved in arranging my journey home.

I had a pressing question, as soon as all the travel arrangements had been given, I had the chance to ask it.

"We haven't been told about where the children we rescued from the coffee plantation are to be taken and what guarantees for their future safety and wellbeing have been put in place."

A member of the Embassy staff answered. "The children were transferred to a known and well trusted orphanage during your trip to St. Lucy. DNA testing is being carried out to ascertain if any of the children had originally been abducted, checking missing child reports is vital and matching possible parents to the children, with DNA matching the ultimate confirmation. Any of the children who are declared genuine orphans will stay at the orphanage, but please be assured it is a bone fide orphanage and the children will receive the highest standard of care."

I thought of all the little darlings, and desperately hoped they would be reunited with loving parents, but I had to face the hard fact that there was only a slim chance of that outcome happening.

And If they could ill afford to support their children previously, how would they now? A change in their circumstances nigh on impossible. That was when I raised the possibility of sponsorship. I'd toyed with the idea since the rescue, my overwhelming need to continue contact and to offer financial support uppermost in my mind.

The rest of the debrief covered the need for secrecy concerning William, King and his teams' participation with the arrests on the island. In summary we had to keep our mouths shut about virtually everything.

That left enough time for us to say fond farewells to Daniel, David and Raul. We swapped email addresses, there wasn't a cat in hells chance that we wouldn't stay in touch, we'd been through too much together, to simply disappear from each other's lives.

Finally, we all thanked King and Payne profusely, acknowledging our huge debt of gratitude for their incredible handling, planning just everything. No swapping of details with those two. They would simply slip back into their world of secrecy, subterfuge and inherent danger. But they would be forever heroes in our eyes.

After all that, I only had time to go grab my belongings from the bedroom. As I hurriedly packed my belongings I took a few moments to glance at the bed, still not quite believing I'd made love with Christian on it.

Then it was straight to the inner courtyard where the ubiquitous large dark SUV with blacked out windows awaited to whisk Christian and I to the airport.

Fortunately, my prayer was answered and the trip was spent mostly in silence. The only acknowledgement of a new dimension to our relationship being Christian's insistence on holding my hand for the whole trip.

It was a whirlwind end to this epic journey.

Now for the hardest of goodbyes as we stood inside Miami airport before parting ways and heading to our departure gates. We embraced each other. Not the embrace of times past, of friends, this time it felt oh so different. A feeling of panic swept through me, then utter desolation.

I fought the tears that threatened to spill out, as Christian took my face in his hands and kissed me, pouring years and years of unrequited love into that one kiss, before pleading with me, "Make your choice soon my love."

It took a gargantuan effort for me to nod, I turned and headed for the gate, not daring to look back.

I knew in my heart of hearts what my decision would be.

To be continued